W9-BXM-757

DETROIT PUBLIC LIBRARY
3 5674 00752351 8

The Merrymaid

Also by Mollie Hardwick

THE SHAKESPEARE GIRL
I REMEMBER LOVE
MONDAY'S CHILD
WILLOWWOOD
LOVERS MEETING
THE DUCHESS OF DUKE STREET
UPSTAIRS, DOWNSTAIRS

The Merrymaid

Mollie Hardwick

St. Martin's Press
New York

 For information, address St. Martin's Press, 175 Fifth Avenue, New York, N.Y. 10010.

Library of Congress Cataloging in Publication Data

Hardwick, Mollie.
The merrymaid.

I. Title.
PR6058.A6732M4 1985 823'.914 85-1715
ISBN 0-312-53019-6

First published in Great Britain by Methuen London Ltd.

First U.S. Edition

10 9 8 7 6 5 4 3 2 1

FOR JULIAN:

Himself a minstrel

CONTENTS

'I have a song to sing, O!'

'What is your song, O?'

'It is sung with the ring
Of the songs maids sing
Who love with a love life-long, O!
It's the song of a merrymaid, peerly proud . . .'

W. S. Gilbert: THE YEOMEN OF THE GUARD

The Merrymaid

After the death of her father, young traveling entertainer takes to the open road alone, falls in love with a handsome young minstral and braves the perils of sixteenth century England.

The heavy ash stick came down once, twice, and the man on the ground lay still at last. He had put up a good fight, being young and agile, but it was three against one. Those who had killed him stood back, eyes eager for anything of value they might have left on him. It had not been a bad haul: a knife with a wrought handle, a gold chain (it was brass, but they would not know that until they tried to sell it), a pouch gratifyingly full of small coin, and a cloak. The cloak was a gaudy thing of good cloth dyed three colours, black, blue and yellow, but some apish lad would fancy it to peacock about in.

'The wench?' The tallest of the three had his eyes on the clump of trees which hid the girl who had fled from them.

'No time. Have done.' The others were already on the run, making for the track that would lead them away from the high road where their victim would be found. He was past being able to describe them, and the girl had shrieked gibberish at them – most like she was a foreigner or a Gyppy.

Jacquette waited in the spinney a full five minutes after the three were out of sight. She was trembling uncontrollably, even the muscles of her face twitching with shock. She struck her cheek a blow, to still it, and to hurt herself because she had run away. When the men had first set on them she had fought like a cornered cat, but to those burly rogues the kicks and cuffs of a child of eleven were no more than feathers. Then her father, felled to the ground, had cried '*Echappe-toi!*' and she had obeyed him and run for cover. They would have killed her too, and what good would that have done? Yet she was bitterly angry with herself that she had not been able to defend him, to mark the *scélérats*' ugly faces for life.

Her mind flew to savage punishments for them – they should

hang in chains until they starved and froze, they should be broken on the wheel, as they would be in France, foul murderers, *coupe-jarrets. If* they had murdered him. She was able to move now, cautiously at first, then running across the frozen ground and lumps of snow to where Estienne Valency lay, his face turned up to the winter sky. Blood had poured from a wound to his head and soaked his leather jerkin from neck to waist – that would be why they had not troubled to strip him for it. His eyes were open, staring, so she knew that he was dead; she had seen plenty of corpses in the streets of Paris, beggars and men killed in brawls. In life he had not been tall, in death he seemed to have shrunk to boy-size. He who had been vivid as a flame, dancer, acrobat, musician, juggler, proud descendant of the old *trouvères*, the troubadours, lay now like a broken puppet.

Jacquette looked down at what had been her dear friend and companion, as well as father and partner. Then she knelt, touched an icy hand and put back a lock of dark hair from the brow. When the two riders came round the slope of the hill they found her so, like a tomb-effigy of Our Lady in a *pietà*.

She hardly noticed what they were like, these elderly citizens who were asking her questions and becoming increasingly exasperated because they could not understand her whispered, toneless replies. Even in her trance of grief, she knew that they were asking how the dead man had met his end, who he was, where those were who had killed him. In her travels with Estienne she had picked up a fair smattering of English words, but now she could not utter a single one of them. These men spoke with the accent of Kent, which was familiar to her, yet she could not answer.

'Pedlars, by the dress,' said one, 'them that counterfeit to be Egyptians and talk their own cant to deceive honest men. They're hot-headed and quick to quarrel, it's said. You, wench,' he addressed Jacquette loudly and slowly, 'did – you – kill – this man? A jealous mistress, mayhap,' he suggested to his companion. 'A mort, or doxy, as they call 'em.' He was somewhat proud of knowing these underworld terms.

His question had been shocking enough to unlock Jacquette's tongue. '*Non, non, non.*' She shook her head violently. '*C'est mon père.*'

A man of Dover could hardly fail to recognise the language, now that he could hear the words. Calais, that noble battlemented seaport, still belonged to the English crown, an important jewel, for it dominated the Channel and looked across to Dover; on a fine sunny day, it was said, you could see their windows shining. Dover and Calais were like neighbour gossips, beldams sometimes fond, sometimes fratching. Dover had its *Maison Dieu*, Calais its Love Lane and Cock Lane and citizens with such names as Pye, Porter and Brown. Only ten years earlier, Calais had sent its most skilful swordsman to remove Queen Anne Boleyn's head from her shoulders.

Yet Master Fagge, for such was his name, could not speak one word of French. Abandoning any attempt to question Jacquette, he informed Master Greene, his fellow-merchant, that the girl said she was of France, and that the dead man was her father.

'Ah. It came to me that she hadn't the years on her to be a – what you said – poxy, was it?'

'Doxy. Well, no matter; what's to be done with her?'

They contemplated Jacquette, who had now risen to her feet. She would be of a seemly height when she was grown, by her long limbs, but now was small and thin, even to scrawniness. Her sharp-featured little face was white under the raw redness the wind had stung into it, her eyes were dark as the sightless ones of the man at her feet, and the long black hair that she was proud of dragged back and crammed into a net caul with a woollen hood over it. Her skirt was short, as it must be for tramping the roads, showing thin ankles and trodden-down shoes. The cloak that covered her was of an unbecoming black: very fortunately for her, she wore it reversed, the tricolour side hidden that would have drawn the robbers' eyes.

What was to be done with her, indeed? Unthinkable that either of the men should take this disreputable waif home, to scandalise his good wife and infect his children with who knew what foreign diseases. 'To my mind,' Master Green observed, 'she might most fitly be called a vagabond, and as such should be taken before the Constable and thrown into gaol, there to be examined as to her means of livelihood.'

But where would they find the Constable, or any of the Watch, at this late hour of a December day, with darkness not far off, and both of them with a shipment of goods to inspect down at the quay? The solution occurred to Master Fagge. 'She shall go to the castle.'

It towered above them, crowning the heights as it had done since the Romans built a lighthouse there to guide their ships round the foreland. The lighthouse was still there, the oldest ruin in England, dwarfed to pepper-pot size by the huge fortress built by the Conqueror, an armed city bristling with towers, threatening land and sea. Jacquette and Estienne had passed it as they came down into Dover, and she had thought it a grim terrifying place, without the grace of the French châteaux, which, compared with it, were most courtly and pleasant. It resembled more the Bastille and the dreaded Châtelet.

Now she was on her way to it, on the crupper of Master Fagge's saddle with her arms clutching his waist, terrified of slipping off over the hindquarters of his massive horse, for her hands were so cold that there was almost no feeling in them. The two men talked as though she were not there. They had done their duty, they agreed, in dragging the corpse to the side of the road, out of the way of hooves and wheels, and disposing it decently. Someone from the castle would go down and see that it was duly taken to the Coroner for an inquest, then given Christian burial. Jacquette caught the last words, and was thankful at least for that.

Then she began to feel rather ill, from cold, fear and shock, and the trembling set in again. Master Fagge, feeling her hold weaken, muttered an oath, reined in the horse, and transferred her, half-fainting, to the saddle in front of him, where he gripped her with no gentle hand until the top of the hill was reached, and they were across the moat and entering the castle by the Constable's Tower.

They were in a courtyard, lanterns dancing against the growing dusk, voices, men shouting and laughing. Jacquette did not understand the jokes that were being made about Master Fagge's baggage and French crowns, and would not have cared if she had. It was like arriving at Hell-mouth, except that she was bitterly cold and the devils were armed with pikes, not pitchforks.

One of the devils seemed to have been put in charge of her. A large soldier had taken her hand (which disappeared entirely in his huge one) and was leading her through a doorway into the castle itself, along a winding stone corridor with flambeaux on the walls at intervals, until they came to a small room down three steps, down which he guided her. Miraculously, there was a fire burning brightly in a grate.

There was something about her escort which calmed any fears Jacquette might have had when he removed her hood and cloak (whistling with surprise at its colourful reverse side) and sat her down on a joint-stool close to the fire. Her hair fell dankly about her shoulders, as though she had been taken out of a pond, half-drowned. The soldier, Ralph Martyn, had heard a chopped-down version of her story, passed on from Master Fagge. He had seen service in France, and picked up a good many useful words and phrases; but the time for talk was not yet.

Jacquette found herself being wrapped from head to foot in a horse-blanket. Its smell was not unpleasant, and its texture thick and comforting. While she gradually thawed within its folds, Ralph heated ale in an iron pan, stirred some spice into it, and invited her dumbly to drink it. Its heat flowed through her body, its powerful fumes rose agreeably to her brain. For the first time since the tragedy of the day she smiled, a charming three-cornered smile that transformed her face and captivated the man, who had so far thought her somewhat like a young rat.

'*Merci, m'sieur,*' she said softly, and was pleasantly astonished when Ralph replied, '*Plaisir, demoiselle.*' The accent was execrable, the manner kind and courteous; and Jacquette had been brought up to regard courtesy as a high virtue. It was the beginning of a conversation so halting that it came at times to a complete stop, neither party having the least idea how to convey its meaning. But from it Ralph gathered that the girl and her father had come to England from Paris at the suggestion of a friend of Estienne's, a musician at King Henry's Court. Jacquette could not quite make him understand why the enterprise had not been successful. Estienne was an accomplished *jongleur*, an entertainer of many talents, and his daughter, young as she was, had been well trained in the same arts. Her mother was dead, they were not rich, and it was said that good money could be made in England where there were few but clowns to entertain a king.

But the time was ill-chosen. King Henry was out of sorts, suffering constant pain from his ulcerous leg. He was also still smarting from his disappointment in his fair young queen Catherine Howard, whom he had been obliged to have beheaded for wantonness, and not yet wedded to a new wife. Once a ready audience for any kind of joyaunce, he was now in no mood for French foolery. It took only an ill-advised choice on Estienne's part – the singing of a song about one Caterina, who came to an unfortunate end – to cause an exceptionally loud royal roar and a fat finger pointing the minstrels to the door and out of his Court.

So there was nothing for the Valenceys to do but earn what they could by performing at the houses of such courtiers as had liked them, and, when they had been seen and heard by all who mattered in London, to return to France. Their takings had been very satisfactory, and in Paris at least they would be able to boast of having performed for *le roi Henri*, who only allowed the best to entertain him.

They had travelled by easy stages to Deal, had been well lodged there near the King's castle (which was built in the shape of a Tudor rose, not formidably like Dover). Then, for the first time, they had failed to find a carter who would carry them by wagon to the port; so they had walked the eight miles in biting cold, singing to pass the time. At the top of Castle Hill they had rejoiced when the harbour came in sight, the sea that would take them home.

Jacquette stopped and shuddered violently. Her hearer, who had been struggling along in the wake of her words, knew that she had reached the point when the robbers had leapt out and set on them.

'*Je,*' he began, '*je savvy la chose que*. That's to say, I was told of the villains' killing of your father. No need to . . .' he laid a finger on his lips and shook his head. She nodded, grateful that she would need to say no more.

'*Vous avez* baggage – gear?' he asked.

'*Non, m'sieur, ma bourse seulement.*' She indicated a leather pouch slung at her belt. Their performance-clothes and apparatus had been left behind in London, to be conveyed to Paris by a friend they had made who would be travelling there by coach.

Ralph regarded her sombrely. To be without possessions was a grave offence in Henry's England. Fulbert de Dover's old tower in the castle was full of debtors who would be allowed to die there unless they could, literally, raise enough money by letting down bags on ropes to charitable passers-by, for contributions. The laws against vagrancy were harsh; they included ear-cropping, branding, whipping and death if the vagrant were stubborn enough to be three times found away from his own parish.

Surely they would not do that to her, a child without kin, though a sharp one, and a stranger in the land. She should rather be treated as the widow and the orphan were, with pity; yet what would be her fate, even so? Perhaps to serve in some citizen's household as a menial, for there were no convents now, since the King had abolished them and turned the nuns on the streets. Ralph had not understood what she had said about performing at Court, but he had vaguely gathered that she could dance and sing and such mummery, which could only put her in danger of her virtue, alone in a strange town.

He was aware of voices in the corridor behind him, crowding heads and lewd gestures, as his comrades scrutinised Jacquette and offered suggestions which he was glad she could not understand. One, a small skinny fellow known as Goat, wriggled under another's arm to confront her, leering with signs of invitation. Jacquette met his grimaces with a stare of complete blankness, the look she had been trained to turn on any who attempted *grossièreté* or *impudicité* towards her. Ralph bundled the man out, roared at the others, and returned to contemplate Jacquette.

'What must I do with you?' he asked her. The girl was in his charge until she could be turned over to the Constable; he was responsible for her safe keeping. Soon he must go on guard duty. To leave her here would be to invite further invasions from comrades with fewer scruples than he; to confine her in Fulbert de Dover's tower with the debtors was undesirable. A solution came to him. Beckoning, he led her through a maze of stone passages, up steps and down them again, until they arrived at a low doorway. Behind the stout oak door was a small room which appeared to have no particular function. It was littered with weapons, '*Too cassy,*' said Ralph, hoping to convey that they were all broken and not dangerous. There were pieces of furniture, also in need of mending, a table and stools with missing legs, and a rough pallet bed. It was a room into which people threw things when they could think of nothing immediate to do with them; which was Jacquette's own case.

Running out of pidgin French, Ralph signed to her to sit on the bed, and indicated in pantomime that he would fetch her food. When it came, cooled from its long journey from a distant kitchen in the barrack quarters, it proved to be rabbit stew. To Jacquette it surpassed anything she had ever tasted at a banquet. Ralph watched her eat it voraciously, with satisfaction.

'*Je vay,*' he said, '*garday,*' and attempted a mime of marching up and down on sentry duty. Jacquette clapped softly, nodding and smiling. Before leaving the room, Ralph paused at the door and let his gaze range round it, as though checking its safety. His eyes rested for a long moment on the back wall, compelling Jacquette to look in that direction. In the shadows thrown by his lantern was another door, low and inconspicuous.

'*Bon swar, ma demoiselle,*' he said. '*Dormay beong.*'

Jacquette bent her head. '*Et vous, m'sieur.*' It was only courtesy to answer in French.

Her friend was gone, and she was alone in the little lumber-room. There was much to think about. Grief for her father, sharp though it was, must wait; there would be a time to mourn, but now was the time to save her own life. He had loved her much and been proud of her; he would not have wished her to throw away all that she was, all that she had been taught.

The soldier had been kind. He was a good man, it was evident, but how many of his fellows were as good? Jacquette knew about men and their propensities. Her soldier would perhaps not be able to take care of her tomorrow, and those who would might be less trustworthy than he. They might keep her in prison, or set her among people who would use her ill, and take away the freedom she loved.

Besides, she followed an honourable profession, and that would be wasted. She opened the pouch and looked at its contents. Two or three English coins, a little dagger with the hilt carved like a crucifix, a silver spoon, a tiny wooden angel with the features rubbed flat because she had played with it since her infancy. Not much. Estienne had carried the rest.

Certainly not enough to get her back to France. At the quay there would be questions, English questions, which she would not be able to answer, and that would lead back to the castle, or worse.

Lantern in hand, she went to examine the other door. It seemed to have no means of opening, neither keyhole nor latch, nor were there any bolts. A mysterious door. Yet, where a door existed, there must be a way out. Jacquette's brain was working busily. One of Estienne's cleverest juggling tricks had been to let himself be tied up, hand and foot, by cords, so that he looked like a trussed fowl; then, inch by inch, he would wriggle out of his bonds until they fell off him and he leapt to his feet and bowed to a wondering audience. Oh, my father, help me, lend me your good wit! she prayed.

Perhaps the soul of Estienne was not very far above her on its journey to the skies, for, in a moment or two, there came into her mind a picture of the door as it might be on the other side. No bolt, for who would bolt a door except from within, to fortify it? No ring-handle, or a lock would have been visible. At one side of the door was a gap, almost half an inch between the edge of it and the stone wall. Jacquette laid her hand against it; a shaft of air much colder than the temperature of the room came from it.

The dagger, said Estienne's voice, try the dagger. She took the little thing from her pouch and thrust the point through the gap; it met no resistance on the other side. Bending, she drew it slowly upwards, alert for anything it might touch. Almost at her shoulder-height it stopped: something was there, something that crossed the gap between the door and wall.

She put both hands to the dagger and forced it upwards. Slowly, very slowly, the object outside rose with the blade, higher and higher – it could only be a latch. When it seemed to go no further upwards, Jacquette forced her fingers into the crack and pulled hard. The door was stiff, heavy, but it was also rotten with age. To her joy, it reluctantly creaked open.

There was no passage, no room beyond; only the dark chill of a December night. The little lumber-room was in a cluster of buildings added higgledy-piggledy to the ancient fabric of the castle. Nobody had troubled to make the door fast on the outside, any more than if it had been a fuel-store or a kennel. The castle was not under siege, the country not at war. Some thought of all this had been in the soldier Ralph's mind.

Jacquette took a deep reviving breath. Then she knelt and sent a brief fervent prayer to *Nôtre Dame* and her precious Son for protection in her hazardous flight. 'I am very young, my body is tired and my spirit in deep sorrow for my father, but I am strong and I have courage. By Your help I escaped from the clubs of the robbers – lead me now through the dangers of this night, and when I can afford it You shall have a thousand candles each, and a thousand more to Sainte Catherine.'

With that, she replaced the lantern inside (it would never do for her soldier to be accused of stealing it), shut the door behind her and set out on her journey.

II
The Angel and the Hermit

The same good fortune which had been with Jacquette in the castle aided her outside it. Instead of total darkness, a frosty moon slid in and out of clouds, revealing open ground sprinkled with caked snow. No fences or walls were between her and freedom, no sentry was in view. She moved away from beneath the bulk of the castle, hoping to see something that would tell her where she was.

It was there, in a long unbroken spell of moonlight: the sea, dull silver, and a glimpse of town roofs, told her that she was on the side of the castle away from it, almost back on the road that had brought them from Deal. Jacquette made for where it must lie, roughly north-west, moving quickly, used as she was to unlit streets and dark stretches of country. (But there was no father's hand to grasp if her foot slipped, now.) Sooner than she could have hoped, the uneven ground gave way to a rutted surface that could only be the road.

There had been civil folk in Deal, where they had lodged in a house near Deal Castle, in Sea Valley. One of the cockle-gatherers had given the foreign child some of his newly-dressed cockles, which she had eaten with pleasure, and the woman of the house had told Estienne and his daughter a long tale of Queen Anne of Cleves landing on Deal beach, hung all over with gold and jewels under rich furs, but green from the tossing of the ship that had brought her from Calais. The gossips had said then that she would never please the King unless the air of London mended her complexion, and they had been right. The little fishing-village had been interesting to the Valenceys, who knew no more of the sea-coast than busy Calais. Jacquette thought she would like to go back to Deal, if only they would not take her up for vagabondage. The walk of eight miles would take all night; a clock in the castle had boomed out midnight before her escape.

The first milestone was past in what seemed no time at all. Then the moon turned sullen, blackness closed in, and unpleasant visions came to flit in Jacquette's mind of devils, ghosts, monsters and wild beasts. Mopping, mowing, grinning, they came at her like bats out of the darkness, as clear as nightmare scenes in the moment before waking. She stumbled along, sobbing, dry mechanical sobs of fear and loneliness. Better to have stayed in the castle lumber-room, trusting to God and the kind soldier, than take this hellish journey, growing colder and more tired at every step. There might be robbers, evil men like those who had killed Estienne, waiting to fall on night-travellers. They would kill her and rob her corpse, all for a silver spoon, a wooden toy and a dagger and only enough coins to buy a loaf. Poor takings; yet her soul would be on its way to Purgatory, perhaps in time to catch up with Estienne's, so they could suffer the torments hand in hand . . .

She was recalled from these unpleasant broodings by noticing, seawards, a faint lightening of the sky, and just visible against it the outline of a building. Instinctively, she turned away from the road and made for it. Whatever it was, there would be a barn or outhouse where she could take shelter until the night was over.

The rough cart-track beneath her feet gave way to grass-land, easier to walk on, sloping downwards sharply. The building was nearer, more discernible. It was a church, though a very small one. At each end of the roof was a stone cross, and the triple-arched windows belonged to no secular buildings. At one end was a mass, difficult to make out from a distance; as Jacquette neared it she saw that it was a ruin, but of what? A confusion of bricks and stone, merely, piled up and scattered as though a thunderbolt had fallen. Jacquette hoped that some outbuilding where she could rest might lie beyond them, and made her way round them to the point where they seemed to stop, some fifty feet from where they joined to the little church.

There was nothing beyond: nothing but sky and sea and the edge of a cliff. But for walking warily she would have gone over it.

Crossing herself, she retreated to safety. The sky was lightening every minute, though with a cold lurid glow nothing like sunrise. She could see now that the little church, no more than a chapel, had a shabby, battered look, though the stone mouldings round windows and door were fine, and the stained glass intact. Jacquette approached the door, hardly daring to hope that it would open and yield some shelter. Yet who would lock a church? She turned the huge iron ring, and the heavy studded door began to open.

The interior was all in darkness. Gradually she began to make out the shapes of table tombs, an altar, with a high painted altarpiece behind, a timber-trussed roof, a great beam across it bearing a crucifix. The building was, indeed, a chapel, without a chancel. Most strangely, there were no candles burning. Jacquette had never before entered a church unlit by pyramids of candles, each before a holy image, golden points of light in a scented gloom. Here was no scent, or sweet lingering fragrance of incense; only stuffiness and a miasma of damp.

Jacquette shivered, pulling her cloak tightly round her. She wished the soldier had not taken her hood. Near the door was a large chair with a back and arms, made for some stately personage, perhaps. She sat down thankfully. Her legs and feet ached miserably, and she had never been so cold, yet it was warmer within than without; she fell into a light doze.

When she woke with a start the light was growing, showing her the chapel in all its stony beauty. The walls were painted all over with Scriptural scenes in brilliant colours and gilding; carved saints stood between the windows, in which each pane was beginning to glow with ruby and sapphire, topaz and emerald. The altarpiece now appeared as a great painting of Christ in Glory, crowned on a throne topping the golden orb of the world, one hand stretched towards His Mother, kneeling adoringly at one side, the other reaching out to St Mary Magdalene, half-hidden in her rich flowing hair. Jacquette got up stiffly to inspect the picture more closely, and fell heavily over a bundle that lay on the floor in front of the altar.

Her cry of *'Ah Dieu!'* produced a faint stirring from within the bundle. As she lay on the floor beside it, winded from the fall, the folds of greyish cloth changed shape, ebbed and flowed, until they slipped gently off like a snake's sloughed skin. With a prolonged yawn, the person who had been inside them sat up.

Jacquette saw a man so thin that he might have been an animated *Memento Mori*, the skeletal shape carved below tombs to remind one that earthly glory was but mortal. He could have been any age, up to extreme eld. Sharp cheekbones almost pierced the skin, dull eyes looked out from cavernous sockets. An unpleasant waft of dirt and neglect came from him, causing Jacquette to wrinkle her nose as she rose from her undignified position to her knees.

Thus, the first thing the sleeper saw was a girl so delicate in feature as to suggest that she fasted much, so dark of eye and hair that she must be other than English: perhaps a child of Rome or the Holy Land. Her cloak was not English, either, but a thing of bright colours like the wall-paintings. She was, he concluded happily, a heavenly apparition come to comfort his loneliness, a reward for all his prayers and penances. Father Robert bent his tonsured head and crossed himself: '*Ave sancta beatissima,*' he said reverently, '*Angelus qui me infelicem apparet.*'

Jacquette had no more Latin than was to be expected of a female, but enough to gather that she was being addressed as a saint and an angel. The poor man was mad, clearly, but he was also a priest, perhaps an anchorite, and such were given to visions and delusions. She smiled. '*Non, mon père, je suis femme, toute mortelle. Ni sainte, ni ange.*'

Father Robert had no French. He took her words to be some holy language, more melodious than earthly speech, though it seemed odd that a heavenly being did not speak Latin. He replied with a prayer in that language addressed to Our Lady, which seemed to him the most appropriate for this visitant.

Jacquette resorted to mime to convince him of her earthiness. She lifted her feet one by one, displaying her worn, wet shoes, then laid her hands on her stomach, making a pitiful face. 'Food!' she said. 'Er, *panis, pabulum. Vide humilitatem meum,*' she added in a burst of inspiration, thankful that Estienne had given her such a sound education at the hands of the good Père Nicolas, just in case circumstances ever forced her into a nunnery: he had taught her some of the Psalms of David.

Father Robert looked puzzled. But it was not for him to question divine commands. Genuflecting backwards from the altar, he opened a small door in a corner of the south transept, stepped outside, and returned bearing a leather bottle, a manchet loaf, two cooked pigeons and a piece of salted meat. Kneeling before Jacquette, he held out these offerings with a humble look. Hardly able to keep her hands from tearing the food and stuffing it into her mouth, Jacquette thanked him prettily, gestured towards a low coffer that stood by the wall, and, as he seemed not to know what to do, briskly laid out the food on it, took a handful herself, and indicated smilingly that he should do the same.

Still puzzled, he nibbled a morsel of the bread. Poor man, she thought, he hardly eats – no wonder he looks so sadly *en squelette*. Then she devoted herself to eating, and to sampling the very good, very strong ale in the bombard. Satisfied at last, a heavy inclination to sleep came over her. She mimed it, and Father Robert eagerly spread the rough blanket he had slept in himself on the floor by the wall. She lay down on it, pulled it round her head, though it smelt vilely and was not free from lice, and fell into the sleep of exhausted youth.

When she woke pale sunlight lit the coloured windows. The priest was kneeling beside her, his gaze fixed on her face; she guessed that he had knelt so all the time. Completely refreshed, she scrambled to her feet, to see him advance to the altar. There he said mass, Jacquette following him throughout from the *Kyrie* to the *Agnus Dei*. When it was finished, Jacquette continued to kneel in prayer, her thoughts full of her father, and gave thanks for the guidance that had brought her to this place.

It came to her that with perseverance some understanding could be reached between the priest and herself. Very deliberately, using sign-language with her eloquent hands, she asked him, in the few English words she knew, to tell her of himself, of how he came to be in such a chapel, and to speak very slowly. He bowed his head, comprehending. This was the story he told her; with all her quick mind concentrated on his words, she understood much of it.

'Many years ago, dear holy child, I was appointed priest to the family of Brandon, who lived in the great house that stood by this chapel. They had built the chapel for their priest in the time of King Richard, in gratitude for the continuance of the

House of York. The priest lived for many years, and when at last God took him I came here as a very young man. That would be – let me see, in the year 1520, when our King Henry was still one of the faithful – alas, alas.

'The family treated me like one of themselves, and I was more than content. They were many – little children, young maids and men, Sir Piers's ancient father and others of the family who came to live under his roof. I thought, by the blessing of God, I should live and die in their service. But then -' Father Robert's face was contorted with remembered pain, 'on a terrible night of storm the calamity came upon us; the cliff on which the house was builded crumbled and fell into the sea, taking a part of the house with it.' He shook his head, thinking of the warnings that had been given to Sir Piers that just such a thing might happen, since his ancestor had been rash enough to build so trustingly close to the cliff edge. But nobody could have foreseen such a great collapse of the chalky soil, the worst within the memory of man.

And so, he ended, what with loss of life and belongings, the Brandons were scattered amongst various lodgings until a new house could be built. He, Father Robert, went to the monks of Christ Church in Canterbury until the day in 1540 when the heavy hand of King Henry fell on all the religious houses in the land and seized their treasures, including Canterbury's great jewelled Shrine of St Thomas, and compelled all clerics to take the oath affirming that the King, and not the Pope, was head of the Church in England.

Monks and nuns had been turned out into the world to beg their bread and live as they could, or die of starvation. Some – the lucky ones – had been pensioned off. Others, like the Abbot of Reading, had been hanged, drawn and quartered.

'I could not have taken the Oath, for my soul's sake,' Father Robert said sadly, 'but my body was too cowardly and weak to face the terrible cruel end I should have if I refused. So I left at night, and walked back to my old home. The house was in ruins, but my chapel was as you see it, dear holy child.' He looked round it affectionately. 'Thieves had broken in and stolen benches and any valuables they could find. But after I came they never stole again. Nay, the people about here use me very kindly, bringing me food and drink, as you saw. I suppose it is because they know I am mad, and mad men are sacred.' For a second a look glittered in his eyes that frightened Jacquette, as though a devil had glanced out of them.

But there was no use in being frightened by Father Robert, even if his ways were sometimes strange. It was important to use this refuge for composing herself to face the new life she would have to live now that Estienne was gone, and the first thing to do was to make herself mistress of the native speech.

'English,' she told the priest, 'you – speak – English – to me.' He did so, after that, in his slow dreamer's voice, much easier to follow than the fashionable chatter of London courtiers. Because the best way to learn a language is to be forced to speak nothing else, and because her brain was bright and her learning-power great, she was soon at no loss for words, even if her grammar was unusual. One of Father Robert's virtues was that he never laughed at any of her mistakes; indeed, he never laughed at all. Jacquette felt it her duty to recall him to some kind of normal life, even though the situation they were in was far from normal. Since he had told her sensibly enough the story of his own life, he had lapsed into great troughs of silence, being unused to anything like conversation. When forced to talk, his attention would stray, and he would often wander away in mid-sentence, to kneel for hours at a prie-dieu, or lie prone in self-abasement in front of the altar.

Every morning Jacquette opened the little door and cautiously retrieved the food left outside. Obviously in the past many of such offerings had never been brought in, but left to rot or become the sustenance of the seagulls who swooped around the chapel continuously. Jacquette was careful to shut the door quickly after bringing the food in. Tongues would wag, even in such a lonely place, and the hermit's benefactors might feel a little less friendly if they thought he had a wench with him. Heaven knows, thought Jacquette, one is as safe with this poor man as in a community of nuns, but we live in a wicked world.

There was a fresh loaf daily; how did they think he could eat it all? Eggs, two or three a day, soft creamy cheese which was often pungently over-ripe, but good to eat with the bread. Sometimes the well-wishers left fish, newly-caught, still silver-scaled and bright-eyed. But to eat it raw was not possible, even for a young keen appetite. With a swift prayer for practical assistance from some sensible female saint Jacquette searched the building for a means to make fire.

The clutter of more than sixty years lay piled up against walls and in corners. There were the remains, mouse-nibbled, of the cushions the Brandons had used in the vanished pews, old breviaries, a Book of Hours illuminated by some dead and gone hand, its brilliant colours and gilding spoiled by time and mice, an ancient helmet which had once hung above a Brandon knight's tomb, broken wooden figures of people and animals, a child's hornbook, and other things Jacquette did not recognise. At last, among a heap of litter behind the altarpiece, something came to light.

It was a three-sided box on goats' legs, of iron, handsomely wrought though rusted. The base of it showed signs of burning, and ash – cold how many years ago? – lurked in its corners. Jacquette sat back on her heels with a triumphant crow. The thing was a little brazier, meant to be used on cold mornings at early mass, for the comfort of chilly Brandons. Coals would have smouldered gently in it with only a wisp of smoke, not enough to annoy noses. A noble family with its own priest might have what it would in church, and the English were a chilly rheumatic race. Jacquette cleaned it, dragged it out of hiding, and displayed it to Father Robert, who stared uncomprehendingly.

'You know this, my Father? You saw it *depuis longtemps* – one time?'

He nodded slowly. 'Lady Alicia. She felt the cold.'

'I also feel the cold. *You* also feel the cold. We want fire. You ask, my Father.'

'Ask whom, child?'

'These people, so kind, who bring food. You wait, *de bonne heure*, morning, tell them candles.'

His pale eyes shone. 'Ah, candles! Yes, yes, they will bring me candles, then we can make our devotions as we should. Candles!'

'Devotions, yes, but first food.' Struggling, she managed to convey to him that in order to light candles one must have fire, and that he must ask the food-bearers for some means of making it.

The half-hour or so it took Jacquette to get this into the priest's head was rewarded. From her uneasy bed of old blanket she heard, soon after dawn, the murmur of voices. With the next offerings of food came a bundle of tallow candles and a tinder-box, a gift more welcome than gold or jewels.

From that time, by Jacquette's ingenuity, they were able to cook food on the tiny brazier well enough to eat without recoiling. Father Robert, who would never in a thousand years have thought of making proper use of his free food supplies, began to take a mild interest in them, and even to eat like a person instead of a sparrow, urged on by Jacquette. The result was a noticeable improvement in his mental state, since his brain as well as his body had been under-nourished. He wandered less in his speech, shortened his long spells of self-abasement, and with a rare smile even made very small Latin jokes. Jacquette always laughed heartily to encourage him.

So, for some weeks of winter, continued the curious, companionship of girl and priest. It could not last, she knew, but it was a good and healing time for her. One could live without luxuries, and there were things to do: Father Robert had a few books, mostly in Latin, but there were others which must have belonged to the Brandon family. One, a book of prayers in English, written by hand in an old style of script, was useful for language-learning, though of no great interest; but a printed book of poems, *The Garland of Laurel*, provided a feast of entertainment for even an unskilled reader, with a good lacing of cheerful bawdry among all the pretty words and rhymes. Jacquette longed to know whether some of it meant what it seemed to mean, but instinct advised her that Father Robert was not the man to ask. Good soul, he might not even understand some of the naughty-looking words.

The time came when, going outside for air, Jacquette knew that winter had gone. A new sweetness was in the air, green shoots that heralded wild flowers brightened the ruins of Brandon Court; in the face of the cliff gulls were nesting, and a blue sky looked down, changing the sea's grey face. Jacquette laughed with pleasure. That day she wandered far from the chapel, finding a rough path which led down and down, twisting and turning, until it brought her to a shingly beach, and the sea.

Oh, the sea! After weeks of close confinement, of dirty clothes and skin (for the only water was what they hauled up from a well in what had been the Brandons' garden) it was bliss beyond bliss to throw off every stitch and run, shrieking with delight as much as cold, into the water. Unable to swim (for the Seine of Paris was not a swimmer's river) she had no fear of a tide so mild, lapping gently against the shore. It cleansed her body, then her hair, until she was all one tingle of cleanliness. Dashing back, she soaked her garments, dragged them through the water and rubbed them on the stones, until it seemed that all the vile *poux* that had infested them must be drowned. She wrung the clothes hard before putting them on again, careless of what chill or bone-ache she might catch. Then, singing, she made her way back up the cliff-path.

A boy was coming down, hoping to find a gull's nest with the birds absent, so that he might take the eggs. His mouth fell open in surprise at meeting with a strange creature: a sprite in the shape of a maiden, all dripping wet, her long black hair flowing about her, singing in her high voice a song in a strange language. She bade him 'Good-day', and her accent made him quite sure of what he had suspected. Forgetting the eggs, he ran home to his mother to tell her that he had met a mermaid, a very mermaid. Within hours the story was all round the village of St Margaret's, with the embellishment that the mermaid had had a long green tail.

Father Robert was standing at the door of the chapel looking about him, his face a picture of anxiety. On seeing her returning he almost ran to meet her, with glad cries, which turned to exclamations of horror at her wet state. She comforted him with soothing sounds; poor man, he had thought himself deserted. Then, because she thought it would reassure him, she warmed her sleeping-blanket at the ever-burning brazier and wrapped herself in it. Though she deserved to take harm from her rashness, she took none, and it was only the first of her journeys down to the sea, sometimes by the winding path, sometimes by a longer route. When she met any person she noticed that they would cross themselves and mutter something before hurrying past her. People must have strange customs in this part of the world. But nobody would connect her with the lonely chapel and its hermit; they must merely be afraid of strangers.

Her wanderings perturbed Father Robert. He was still not sure, in his clouded mind, what kind of being he was entertaining, except that he still thought her not to be wholly of mortal kind, even though she ate and slept as others did. But he cherished her above all things, gave thanks daily for her company and the good she had wrought him, and grieved over her ventures into the strange unfamiliar world outside the four stone walls.

Jacquette saw his sadness, and pitied it. She could not give up the freedom of her walks, and the sea, and she would leave him some day, but it troubled her to see him cast down, and she thought of a way to cheer him. But how stupid! Estienne would have thought of it long ago.

'I make you laugh,' she promised. 'I make *jonglerie*, jugglery, you understand? I am *jongleuse, bateleuse.*' Surely he would understand that, especially with a lively pantomime of throwing things into the air and catching them again. Father Robert, who did not in the least understand, nodded, his eyes wide with awe. Jacquette made a little formal bow to him and two more to her imaginary audience. Then she laid out her properties on a stool: four eggs, a handkerchief she had washed in the sea, her little knife, a piece of thin cord. This she stretched out taut, then gave Father Robert the knife and gestured that he should cut it. Nervously he obeyed; the cord fell into two pieces, which Jacquette crushed together in her hand, saying *'Pax, Max, Fax,'* in a mysterious voice, and with a twist of fingers showed him the cord, whole again. Or so it seemed.

Father Robert stared and gasped, ashen-pale. With another bow, some airy gestures, and the words *'Sidonay, Bathin, Eligor,'* Jacquette placed a candle in a rushlight-holder, lit it, and directed her frightened audience's eyes to the wall, on which there appeared in rapid sequence the shadow of a fox eating up a rabbit, a horse running with neck stretched out, and something with sharp ears, very like a devil, smiling; all the work of small sinuous fingers.

'No more, no more!' cried the priest, but Jacquette puffed out the candle, made passes over an egg, then beckoned and coaxed the egg to walk slowly up the candle and slowly down again. Father Robert did not know that the egg was blown and a dark hair from the magician's head threaded through it. His attempt at a prayer turned to a groan, and he fell heavily to the ground in a dead swoon.

III
The Catching of a Mermaid

'Dear Father Robert, calm thyself! Have no more fear, there is nothing for fear . . .' Jacquette held a cup of water to the priest's dry lips, kneeling beside him and supporting his head. But his eyes slid away from hers, and he muttered over and over 'Sorcery, sorcery!'

'It was not *la sorcellerie*, it was *legerdemain*, the quick conveyance of the hand. Oh!' She sighed with exasperation. 'See, I show you.' She exhibited the two halves of the severed cord, then the whole one she had substituted for it. She made him feel the lightness of the blown egg and showed him the hair which had manipulated it, then re-lit the candle and spread her fingers so that he could see that there had been no fox, no running horse, no fiend, only her fingers. But all to no purpose; he only clutched his rosary, his lips moving soundlessly in a prayer against evil. '*Contere brachia iniqui rei,*' he murmured within himself, too terrified to speak aloud, '*et lingua maligna subvertetur.*'

Jacquette left him. She was angry with herself and impatient with the old simpleton's ignorance. Where had he spent his life, not to recognise simple conjuring when he saw it? The atmosphere of the chapel seemed close and oppressive with its odours of dust and smoking tallow. She put on her cloak and went out into the sharp air of the March day. The distant gleam of the sea, glinting under a changeable sky invited her; she made her way down the path. A baby rabbit bobbed out of its burrow in the turf, staring at her with bright bolting eyes. She chirruped to it, a young thing like herself that meant no harm to anyone, and would also be misunderstood.

At the edge of the cold waves she washed her hair and bathed her face and arms, and immediately felt better. Out at sea were small fishing-boats, and beyond the headland, on the infamous

Goodwin Sands, swallower of ships, two skeleton masts showed where a great vessel had found a grave. Looking south-westwards a faint outline of land could be seen: France. Jacquette heaved a deep sigh, and felt her eyes begin to prickle with tears. In France they understood the finer things, the art and charm of *jonglerie*. And there was a story that even *Notre Dame* herself had smiled on a humble acrobat who had nothing but his skills to offer Her . . . *She* would never have made Father Robert's mistake.

But the priest was still on Jacquette's conscience. She looked about for something that might please him, and saw a long branch of bladder-wrack, shining like a dark snake. With that, and a handful of curious shells, she set off on the upward path, rehearsing in her mind English words of explanation, absent-mindedly popping the moist nodules of the seaweed.

To her surprise and alarm, when she reached the end of the path there were people waiting on the cliff-top; some fifteen or twenty, old and young, men and women, rustics by their dress. As she stepped on to level ground, a sort of concerted growl or murmur went up. Eyes bored into her, eyes raked her from head to foot, fingers pointed, mouths moved saying words she did not understand.

' 'Tis the mermaid. Young Wat spoke truth, then.'

'Look, hair down to her tail!'

'She got no tail.'

'She have, then, only 'tis hid.'

'She carries wrack 'stead of flowers.'

'Her skin be green, look!'

Jacquette's face was indeed pale, from fear of these menacing strangers who were closing in on her. There was no way back except down the cliff, and they looked quite dangerous enough to push her from top to bottom. As she glanced desperately from side to side a man stepped forward and seized her. She felt herself held and lifted, carried through the pressing, peering folk, to a place further off from the cliff-edge where they could all gather round and stare, as she lay where the man had dropped her heavily. 'Bind her, bind her fast!' someone cried. She was roughly turned over and her wrists tightly bound with something that cut into them, making her cry out with pain.

'She got a voice! Bean't they dumb, like fishes?'

'Nay, they sings to trap poor sailors. Sing for us, mermaid!'

A foot was prodding her ribs. They were muttering horribly, 'The tail! let's see the tail!' The man who had carried her, and others, thrust each other aside to get close to her. Someone turned her over on her back, so that her bound wrists were painfully pushed against the ground, and to the accompaniment of squeals and snorts of excitement hands pulled up her skirts until she was naked to the waist, her face crimson now with outrage, her protests unheeded.

There was a general groan of disappointment. Two perfectly normal feminine legs could not by even the wildest imagination be construed as a tail.

'A cheat!' cried a woman. 'That's no fish-maid, 'tis as mortal as I be.'

'But prettier, eh, lads?' Rough fingers were touching her obscenely, mauling her flesh until she screamed with pain and shock, aware that the salacious curiosity of those gathered round her was so strong that no woman among them would come to her aid. Greed, lust, cruelty and superstition were written on every face that looked down on her. Estienne had warned her of the shameful things that might happen to a maid; she had even seen them happen in the Paris streets, and now this most shameful thing was happening to her. She shrieked at them every French curse she knew, and they jeered back, mocking and pointing, the savage noise they made growing even louder. She wished passionately that she could die of shame and anger. If only the robbers on Castle Hill had killed her as well as Estienne, and spared her this!

Into the excited clamour a voice broke, clear and loud as the stroke of a bell.

'What *is* this? What are you at?'

Instantly they were silenced. The men, gathered round Jacquette like wasps, drew back and got to their feet. Caps came off and women dipped curtseys.

The personage who stepped into Jacquette's tear-blurred view was tall and upright, richly but plainly dressed, as a prosperous merchant's wife might be. A short camlet cloak covered her shoulders, her farthingale was straight and protected by a linen apron, and her coif was topped by a severe mannish hat. She was neither young nor old, her face high-nosed and handsome. Her voice was as cold as a frozen brook.

'I asked what this is? Murder? Rape? A new form of Lenten mortification? Restore that wench to decency and take her up.'

The man who had been the ringleader spoke, more humbly than before. 'If you please, Mistress Brandon, 'tis no wench, but a mermaid.'

The personage gave a short sharp laugh. 'I am deaf, good people. I thought I heard Dick Vole tell me this unfortunate creature is a mermaid.'

Many voices assured her that this was true. The mermaid had often been seen coming up from the sea, all wet, singing in a strange language, and vanishing no one knew where. She had never been seen before in these parts – the waves must have stranded her. It was not right to leave such an outlandish being free to do harm.

'*You* appeared to be doing harm to *her*. Tell me of that, Dick Vole.'

'We did but search for her tail,' said Vole sheepishly.

'Then you looked too high. Stand up wench, and tell me the truth of all this coil. Who are you?'

Jacquette's knees were trembling, and her English had quite deserted her. '*Je suis française, madame. Mon pere était tué à Douvres, et je me trouve seule en Angleterre.*'

The lady nodded, then addressed the demoralised crowd. 'This is no mermaid or sprite, or whatever you took her to be – if I can believe such louts, such dolts, such eftish hinds and lewd bawcocks as you. I had heard rumours and so bestirred myself to come in search of the truth. I have a mind to tell this to the magistrates, naming each and every one of you for foul behaviour and unlawful doings. This is a child, a French child, cast orphaned on our shore, and deserves all civilness and courtesy, not such facinorous lowting and unproper rudeness as you showed her. You are neither women nor men nor Christians, but beasts, and when Father John hears of this I'll lay a groat he'll ban you from his congregation. Go now, out of my sight, and be thankful I have no whip with me to lay about your backs.'

The crest-fallen faces of her former tormentors gave Jacquette a wild desire to laugh, now that she was on her feet and decent again. Silently they slunk away by ones and twos, as if unwilling to seem to know each other. Mistress Brandon looked after them with a grim smile.

'So much for those blockheads. Now, wench, tell me, and slowly, how you came in this plight.'

Stumbling in a mixture of French and English, Jacquette told her story. When she came to tell of the chapel and Father Robert, Mistress Brandon's face displayed astonishment.

'Father Robert? He that was our priest – chapel priest to the Brandons?'

'*Oui, madame.* He say this.'

'Well, well, well . . .' Mistress Brandon nodded her formidable hat several times. 'Come, let's go.'

At the door of the chapel Mistress Brandon did not pause to knock, but strode in, Jacquette behind her. Father Robert was on his knees. His face was a picture of shock as he saw his visitors.

'Yes, Father Robert, it is Margaretta Brandon,' said that lady, shutting the door and regarding him with reproof tempered with affection. 'You thought never to set eyes on me again, I suppose, you old fox, hiding here? Well, you're found out, so explain yourself.' She perched herself on the stately chair.

'Not hiding, dearest madam . . .'

'What, then? We heard of you at Canterbury after the Beast in Revelations had destroyed our abbeys, then you were gone, none knew where. Folk about here did talk of a hermit living in our poor old chapel – I should have known it would be you, back in your old "den-o, den-o, the fox has run back to his den-o". And what a place!' She gazed round it. 'As many comforts as the condemned hole in the Clink – dark as Erebus – cold as charity. And it stinks – phoo!'

'I made fire,' Jacquette put in, her housewifely instincts outraged.

'Did you, child? Well.' She jumped up and began to range about the chapel, peering into corners, moving things, with sharp exclamations of scorn and disgust. Father Robert paced nervously behind her, anxious to keep close to her familiar figure and as far away as possible from the one who had given him such a fright. At last Mistress Brandon returned, dusting her hands.

'This is an unfit place for you to live in,' she said to Father Robert, 'or for anyone else, for that matter. But what is still more unfit is that you should have dwelt here with this young maid. A priest and a wench together day and night – oh fie! I wonder none of them broke in and stoned you.' As he began to protest she held up a hand. 'No words. You'll tell me she is innocent as a lamb, and I know you to be a babe unweaned in the ways of this world, but the minds and imaginations of men are wicked. We must have no more of it, this huddling like two pigs in a sty. A mercy she was no older, or the scandal would have been great. So –' She seated herself in the imposing chair and delivered judgment.

'Father Robert, you will go with me to the vicar of St Margaret-at-Cliffe, and he shall find a corner for you as curate or what he thinks fit, that is if you can brace up and bear yourself like a man, and not a scabby old church mouse. Lord, Lord! what would Sir Piers think of you now, if he could rise up from beneath the stones?' She pointed to the most recent of the monuments, so dramatically that Jacquette almost expected the robed effigy to climb off his tomb and join them. Mistress Brandon's piercing dark gaze was now turned on her.

'And you, maid, what of you? I tell you without favour that any beggar would spare you his last crust, looking as you do now. A fright-crow, a mawkin, a thing of nought, a draggletail, and scarcely a word of honest English in its mouth – what's to be done with such a poor mammet?'

To Jacquette all this sounded like a severe scolding. She must have offended this alarming person gravely. She was in disgrace, all for something she could not help. Father Robert now feared and shunned her, and she still trembled from her ordeal at the cliff-edge. She dropped her head in her hands and burst into tears.

Margaretta Brandon was not an unkind woman, for all her hectoring manner. For many years she had lived an independent life, with ample money to spare, in a good house where she ruled her servants with a strong hand. She was used to being looked up to, revered, obeyed. Her dead husband, Walter Brandon, had given her her own way in everything. She was lucky in him, for instead of blaming her for her childlessness, as husbands were wont to do, he pitied her for the miscarriages and infant deaths of her early married years. Only Walter had known that Margaretta had shared her life with an imaginary daughter, a being shaped and moulded by her into perfect womanhood, her companion, pride and jewel, future mother of a brood of sturdy little Brandons.

Margaretta's heart was touched by Jacquette's tears, her maternal instincts, already roused, were strengthened, confirming her in what she had in any case decided to do. Behind Jacquette's draggled appearance she discerned a quality of refinement, even elegance, and behind her halting words a quick, trainable mind. Here was the raw material for her moulding, the child she would recreate as her dream daughter. This waif, in her hands, should become a lady bred, if not born.

To have put her arm round the child would have been undignified weakness, but she administered a firm pat to the heaving shoulders, saying in a much softer voice, 'There. Now. Cheerly, cheerly. Never weep, I'll look after thee. *Je serai votre protectrice*, plague take this scurvy French.'

Jacquette lifted her head. She was not, after all, in disgrace. This strange loud lady had kind intentions towards her. She was rich and powerful, she would be a good *protectrice* to have. And after weeks of thin, meagre living in cold and discomfort with the strange priest, Jacquette needed badly to be looked after. She smiled damply, and made to Mistress Brandon the formal bow that she had made to audiences. It pleased Madame, who said, 'Come, we will all go to my house and there you shall be disposed as I think fit.'

Her house was not far, being in the hamlet called after St Margaret, a handsome building of brick and timber set in neat gardens. On the way there Father Robert walked by Mistress Brandon's side, slowly, because walking was an unfamiliar exercise, talking of old times and this and that, and seeming already a more normal and rational creature than the lonely hermit had been. He did not look back at Jacquette; she knew that her rash demonstration of conjuring had ended the curious comradeship they had shared.

When they reached the door of her home, Mistress Brandon hallooed, calling upon any within there to come out. Jacquette turned before following her indoors, and looked back at the green of the cliff-tops, the shining sea whose other shore was France, the rough road-track by which one might travel to Deal and so back to London. Within the house there would be rest, food, warmth, comfort, the way to a new life.

But outside lay freedom.

IV
A Fair, and a Fortune

The old King was dead, a bloated, gross wreck at fifty-five. His only son Edward, a pale, solemn, clever child of ten, was supposedly only a figure-head behind the Protector, Edward Seymour, Earl of Hertford, his uncle, but in fact exercised his own strong will to make his country's Church far broader and more distant from Rome than it had been in his father's time. Masses were on their way out, and the faithful grumbled.

The farmers and land-workers also grumbled, because enclosures were stealing their sheep-pastures away. A summer of heavy rain was looked on as God's vengeance on the King. There was an uprising in the North and everywhere resistance to the unwelcome changes that had come to old England. But daily life went on and holidays were kept as they always had been. The Maypole was decked with ribbons and painted green and white, Whitsun-ale was drunk, lads and lasses went singing into the woods and came home bearing armfuls of flowers, especially the fragrant hawthorn, the flower of May. And in a valley-meadow between St Margaret's and the hamlet of Guston there was to be a fair and all sorts of merry-making.

Jacquette hesitated between the choice of a tawny taffeta gown and another with the green-blue sheen of a peacock's tail. Either would suit her well, she knew. She was sixteen now, a woman grown, neither short nor tall but a comely height, with long legs and a figure that promised buxomness. Her face, once pinched and pale, had filled out into a delicate oval, in which were set a pair of dark brown, thick-lashed eyes which had already slain a good many hearts, and a petal-pink mouth with a slight, seductive pout to the lower lip. Night-dark hair hung down to her waist without curl or ringlet. Her hands were her most remarkable feature, being long and slender, yet of a strength which made them something quite other than the fine useless hands of a lady. Like her face, their skin held a faint tinge of olive. All that remained to show her French origins was her voice, light and quick, still strongly accented.

The five years in Margaretta Brandon's household had been good ones. The misfortunes of the time after her father's death slipped into the past like shadows, leaving no mark. Margaretta had listened to the story of her protégée's life, had shaken her head, and remarked that such was no manner for a decent maid to live, and any French ways of that sort must be forgotten. But she would encourage Jacquette to sing the old songs from her wandering times, *coq-à-l'ânes*, *lais*, *chansons*, ballads quaint, comic and rustic for the road, love songs and conceits for the Court. When the words were none too decorous Jacquette omitted to translate them, for fear of offending Mistress Brandon; but the Englishwoman's knowledge of French was enough to give her the meaning of much that Jacquette politely left to the imagination, and then her gruff laugh would surprise the singer at the virginals.

Mistress Brandon did not approve of conjuring. It was a trade only fit for cozeners and low fellows, she said. Only in her bedchamber, after the old dame who tended her had left her for the night, could Jacquette practise the old skills with kerchiefs and such small things as might be made to appear and disappear and change shape. It was such a pity to lose the art, when one's hands and eyes were trained . . .

She had tried to explain to Father Robert, now a humble curate to the parish priest, about the terrible fright she had given him.

'It was not magic, indeed, Father. I tried to tell you then – it was only a trick, a deceit, merely to amuse. There was no harm in it.'

'The Devil is behind all such tricks, daughter.'

'No, no! There are jugglers who use them to get money from simple folk, but the thing itself is innocent.' (Estienne had not scrupled to take plenty of money from simple folk by the Three Cups trick, but no matter for that.) Father Robert could not be shaken. He would always regard Jacquette as a child of the Evil One who had deceived him, and would never quite believe in her transformation into a sedate English maiden under the Brandon wing.

Just as Jacquette had decided on the peacock gown, with tawny slashed sleeves, her chamberwoman, Dame Annet, entered unceremoniously.

'Eight of the clock and Master Tuke waiting below, and you not dressed yet – fie!' The old lady bustled about with pins and ribbon-points, scolding through toothless gums, while Jacquette shrugged and twitched under her hands. Half of her mind was on the pleasures of the fair on such a golden morning, the other half on her intended bridegroom. Master Gregory Tuke of Deal was nephew to the Master of the King's castle of Sandown, to the north of the fishing village, and his prospective heir. He was twenty-one years old, with a good competence from his own father, a prosperous cloth merchant, and was in need of a wife to give him sons who would be brought up in the business. His relations had hummed and hawed about the alliance of their Gregory with a girl of mysterious antecedents and a foreigner at that, but Margaretta had fixed them with a stern eye while telling them a totally convincing and totally untrue story about Jacquette's birth in a château. Jacquette was not sure that she wanted to be married to Master Tuke, or to anybody, but the matter was not in her hands. Mistress Brandon had decided, a handsome dowry had been agreed, and that was that.

The wedding was to be on Lammas Day, the first of August, a date nicely poised between sheep-shearing and harvest, when a bridal feast would make a welcome interlude, and, with St Swithin's blessing, no rain would fall to spoil the fun. Jacquette would wear a Venice gown of yellow velvet, the nuptial colour, a green petticoat, and a garland of fresh flowers with sprigs of rosemary woven into it. The gown was at present in the making, but not to be finished until just before the ceremony, as the bride was still growing and had an uncomfortable tendency to become taller and plumper from one week to the next. Half-finished and ghostly, it hung over a rail by the bed, giving its future wearer no chance to forget her coming state.

Gregory Tuke was waiting in the parlour, idly calculating the probable cost of the embroidered cushions on Mistress Brandon's day-bed. He intended to have just such fine work in his own house, the best woollens and velvets, handsomely-wrought bed hangings and the like. The house was in a cold position, on the southern outskirts of the town of Sandwich, facing the sea flats and the Small Downs. But it was good healthy stinging air in those parts, which had brought a permanent ruddy glow to his own pleasantly unremarkable face: would that it might encourage the growth of his moustache, at present too scanty to satisfy him.

Jacquette, entering, dipped him a curtsey. She was looking particularly comely in her bright plumage, and he would like to have said something flowery about her nymph-like appearance, but such felicities did not come easily to him. He merely bowed and greeted her. She was the best-looking of any of the young women who had been paraded for his inspection and choice, with a touch of strangeness, a difference, about her which would have fascinated some men with adventurous tastes. Gregory had none, only a keen eye for the width of her hips and bosom, future containers and nourishers of his sons. Daughters, even; a daughter might make a good match that would earn her father social points.

'Your servant, Mistress Valencey.'

'Master Tuke.'

Christian names might come later, or never, both parties remaining on formal terms even in bed. It was the custom in their degree of life, though the humbler might call each other Hodge and Tib.

Her betrothed's arm was stiffly crooked with her hand linked in it as they walked through the people gathered for the fair. The sun had been long up, and everyone not tied to work was there, rejoicing in the sweet May scents, the warm air freshened by sea-salt, the general merriment. The Maypole was dressed, though none were yet gathered round it, for the centre of attention was a white cow, sleek, washed and groomed to perfection. A gilded bell was about her neck, which like her head was garlanded with flowers. She chewed grass and gazed amiably from side to side at the dairy-maids dancing round her, hands linked, to any steps they fancied, while a fiddler played lilting tunes, one after another. A band of children was going round bearing on poles a wooden doll dressed all in white, begging ha'pence for Our Lady. Gregory Tuke shook his head.

'That will cease soon, if the reformers have their way. Already they call such things popish idolatry.'

'What a pity,' said Jacquette. 'She is so charming, with her little gold crown. How can she be an idol?'

'Any set-up image may stand for popery,' he said. 'Think how the priests tricked us for so long, with images that bled scarlet paint and wept tears that came from a bottle. We want no more of that.'

Jacquette sighed. It seemed that one must make the best of the times before they changed too much. 'Let's go and see the Morrisers,' she said. The Morris-men were leaping and flinging to the clink of bells at knees and elbows, the tootling of a flageolet and the beat of a tabor both played by the same versatile musician. Jacquette laughed at them, and the hobby-horse who was frightening the maids by threatening to draw them under his flowing skirts.

Then there was the Learned Pig, already tapping out folks' fortunes with his little hoof, and the Butts set up at the end of the meadow for those that liked to show off their skill in archery. Gregory refused to be drawn towards this, or to the Mask of Robin Hood and his Maid Marian that was beginning, Marian all in red with a clove carnation in her hand, to show that summer had come, and Robin brave in Lincoln green, locked in a mock combat with the fat Franciscan Friar Tuck. Instead, Gregory led his lady to a sweetmeat stall, and there purchased several gingerbread figures ornamented in coloured sugar, which he ate, slowly and methodically, as they strolled about.

Jacquette had come to the fair eager to enjoy herself, pleased with the prospect of having a young man at her side. She had only so far encountered her betrothed in company, in Mistress Brandon's parlour or at the house that would be theirs when they were married, which was full of servants and Tuke relations. He had seemed formal and grave then, but he was young, only four years older than she – he would surely unbend and laugh with her, on this day of May, with merriment all round them. But he had only one manner, it seemed, and it was not a holiday one. A sudden impatience seized Jacquette, and a rebellious anger. She pulled away from the restraining arm.

'Look,' she said, pointing to a distant corner of the meadow, beyond a clump of trees, 'they're setting up the queen's bower. She is my friend Rose Warren – I beg leave to go and talk with her.' Without waiting for such leave, or taking any account of her companion's surprised face, she left him. Rose Warren was not a particular friend of hers – indeed, she rather disliked that flaxen-fair and vastly conceited young woman – but it was necessary to get away if she were not to turn shrewish. She hastened, noting out of the corner of her eye that Master Tuke had returned to the stalls of the food-vendors and was buying sugar mice.

Beyond the trees someone was playing what in France was prettily called a *chifonie*, and in England, less prettily, a hurdy-gurdy. The tune was unknown to her, but, having played it over once, the musician supplied the words in a tenor voice that was light, sweet and clear, as though a chorister had grown to manhood without suffering the mannish crack:

'My love is neither young nor old,
Not fiery hot, nor frozen cold,
But fresh and fair as springing briar,
Blooming the fruit of young desire.
Not snowy white, nor rosy red,
But fair enough for Shepherd's bed,
And such a love was never seen
On hill, or dale, or country green.'

Jacquette advanced, and watched him, now revealed as a group of listeners melted swiftly away when his outstretched cap was proffered. He was as young as he had sounded, slender, no taller than herself. His costume was much like that of the Morrisers, a jerkin of blue with sleeves puffed to the wrists, from which ribbons flew, short round breeches and hose of different colours, one sea-blue, one gold. A leather pouch was slung at his belt. A pain of remembrance twisted Jacquette's heart: Estienne had worn such clothes. The singer's complexion was of a pale brown, which would deepen in the summer sun, and his face a pointed oval, as might be that of Oberon, King of Fairyland. (*Not snowy white nor rosy red*; now, Master Tuke was a permanent rosy red.) A lock of dark hair fell across his forehead from beneath a small cap with a mock jewel at the side.

His non-paying listeners being gone, he laid down the hurdy-gurdy and applied himself to the small table before him, setting out on it three cups made of some dark-coloured glass, and three wooden balls, red, green and blue. Beside these he laid a folded kerchief, a pile of coins, and a small wand. Then he picked up a little tubular trumpet and announced through it, 'Come and see the wonders! Come play the game of Cups and Balls! Come and win your fortune! Maids, money to buy ribbons – lads, money to buy fairings for your lasses. Come play! Come play!'

A few drifted towards him, Jacquette among them. Amused, she watched him pick up one cup and show it freely, then measure the inside with the wand, to show that there was no false bottom, no deception. After doing the same with the second cup, he amazed his viewers by apparently passing the wand right through the bottom of the third. As a gasp of astonishment went up he nonchalantly passed one cup through the other, or appeared to. From this wonder he went smoothly on, arranging the three cups upside down on the kerchief and performing the most amazing feats of deception on the eyes of the audience, whom he challenged, for the reward of a penny, to guess under which cup the red ball might be: but it never was under the one they named. 'Alas, alas, maids! this magic is hard to tilt with.' And so on, through the repertoire, coaxing them to put down stakes, a groat, a ha'penny, without ever winning it back. They stared, they gasped, they admired. Then, satiated with wonder, they left. Only Jaquette remained.

'I saw you palm the white ball last time,' she said. 'You should be a touch quicker, even at the end of the run.'

The conjuror stared. She saw that his eyes were very bright and of a light clear brown, like sherris sack. 'Mistress?'

'And I should let someone win, now and then. A child is best, then they take you for a kind-hearted fellow. If you never lose a coin, then you lose their goodwill. I am surprised you were not taught that.'

'You are surprised,' he repeated slowly. 'Now, *I* am surprised that a fine young lady knows the tricks of my trade.'

'I know them very well,' she said. And then they were saying nothing, but staring at each other like folk transfixed by a spell. I know him, she thought, or I should. But he was not at the Michaelmas Fair, nor at Twelfth Day. She was aware of a curious sensation in her right hand, as though it longed to reach out and trace his features; the sharp points of cheek-bone, with small hollows beneath, the tilt of eyes and winged brows, the fine-lipped mouth that was made for singing and for uttering witty sayings and for . . . She clasped her hands together, tightly uncomfortable, against such waywardness.

And he, who dealt in marvels, wondered at this living one, a well-bred young maid who was neither rustic nor fine lady, and knew the same secrets as he; and who looked at him with what he recognised, though she did not, as the theme of his song – 'Blooming the fruit of love's desire.' He had seen it in the eyes of light-skirts, but this was none.

She broke the spell. 'What is your name?'

'To answer by the Catechism, it is Alan.'

'And for the rest?'

'Thornwood. But I am called Alan-a-Dale.'

'But that is Robin Hood's minstrel.'

Jacquette gestured towards the Mask, which was still going on. 'Why are you not with them, then?'

'I sing their ballads and gestes when needed. But I earn better by plying my own trade – at which, I now learn, I am so feckless. Now you have paid for that unkindness with a blush, Mistress, you shall pay another forfeit and tell me your own name.'

'Jacquette Valencey.'

'So, no Maid of Kent?'

'No, of Paris. My father was a *jongleur*.'

In a few words, a brief exchange, a world had opened up between them, not to divide, but to offer itself for their delighted exploring. They were two of a kind, with so much to say, so much to do, and so little time – for already people were gathering round, hoping for entertainment, wondering at the two lost in each other's eyes. Jacquette felt a sharp tug at her arm, and turned to face her betrothed.

'I thought you were lost,' he said. 'Rose says you have not been near her, and Mistress Brandon waits for you to help her serve out the Whitsun-ale and honey-cakes.' Sure enough, a formidable figure, accompanied by two maids with loaded baskets, was approaching them. 'I hope you have not been taken in by thieves' tricks here.' He raked Alan and the table with a suspicious glance. 'These fellows take all and give nothing; they should be whipped.' Alan acknowledged this pronouncement with a polite bow and a broad wink to Jacquette when Master Tuke had turned away. Jacquette impudently returned it, reflecting that it was she who would get the whipping if Mistress Brandon had happened to notice the exchange. Then, obediently, she took the offered arm and they joined the throng, which was considerable now that all who were free, and some who were not, had come in from hamlets and farms.

There were so many pastimes; Master Tuke made sure she joined in them all, after giving him the slip – dancing, kiss-in-the-ring, throwing hoops for prizes (at which he won a very tawdry bauble, and complained bitterly because it was not worth having), and watching the mummers, who were performing their Mask of Robin Hood all over again with the ludicrously unskilled help of local characters. The mole-catcher of Kingsdown impersonated Much the Miller, a great farm-lad lumbered about as Little John, and two giggling dairymaids minced after Marian as her attendants. Alan was not with them. Jacquette, desperate to talk with him again, peered about the crowds until she saw him, beneath an oak tree, seated at his table. Cards were spread out on it, and he wore a black garment worked with stars, moons and zodiacal signs.

'I must have my fate read,' she said, loudly above the laughter. 'Don't deny me, for I long to know it.' Ignoring Master Tuke's protests, she broke away and made towards Alan, knowing that she would be followed, but better that than nothing.

Alan gave no sign that he knew her, barely glancing up when she said, 'My fortune, if you please.'

'Shuffle the cards, mistress. Shall I show you the way?'

'I'll make shift for myself, thank you.' Neither smiled.

He selected a card himself and laid it face upwards. It was the Queen of Diamonds.

'That is yourself, the Queen. I place her so. Now, if you

please, choose three cards – any you wish, from anywhere. Keep their faces hidden.'

Jacquette, who had so often told other people to do the same, solemnly selected three, looking as awed as she could. Master Tuke was beside her, breathing disapproval, and so, somewhat more alarmingly, was Mistress Brandon. Alan murmured some words which she knew were gibberish founded on dog-Latin. Then he requested her to turn the first card upwards. It was the Nine of Diamonds. He contemplated it, as though deeply reading its message. Then he said, 'You have come from far, you will go far. I see a journey by land.'

It was not quite the standard reading of that card; she waited to see how he would embellish the next, which was the Eight of Hearts.

'I see fine clothes and wealth, but not yours yet. I see a marriage . . .' He paused. 'Children.'

Master Tuke appeared somewhat mollified. He waited for the fortune-teller to mention a handsome good-natured gentleman, upright and noble. Perhaps the fellow would prophesy that Mistress Tuke might one day become My Lady. But at the turning-up of the next card, the Ten of Spades, Alan was silent at first. Then he said 'Gold will come through death. Death at . . . I can see no more.' He turned the card hastily over and reshuffled the pack.

The colour had gone from Jacquette's cheeks. One must never mention death, never, to the customer; it caused fear and gave one a bad reputation. Her new-found friend was very unwise, for he had already roused the wrath of Master Tuke, who had heard nothing at all to his advantage. 'A mountebank, a cursed cheater, a chattering knave!' he cried, dragging Jacquette away, whilst Mistress Brandon harangued Alan for delivering such a croaking fortune to an honest maid with her betrothed in full hearing. 'Let's have no more of your filthy hariolations here, sirrah, or I'll have you whipped and put in the stocks and run out of the parish, mark me if I don't!'

Half-pulled along by the two of them, like a reluctant calf going to market, Jacquette knew that she must speak to Alan again, and that this was her last chance. She was free of both her captors before either knew what was happening, and she could run like a hare. Alan was telling the fortune of a fat wife with children pulling at her skirts. Jacquette pushed them aside, ignoring cries of protest, and asked softly and urgently, 'Do you know the chapel on the cliffs, by the ruined house?'

'I know it.'

'Be there tonight – midnight if you can. Don't fail me.'

He nodded, as though it were not important, and continued to read the cards for his client. 'A husband for your little maid, wife, and sixpence a week for your man . . .'

To Mistress Brandon Jacquette explained untruthfully, 'I had given that lad a whole shilling in mistake for a penny, but he was honest and gave it me back.'

Her guardian snorted. 'There's some honesty in the knave, then, or else he knew I should be as good as my word. Come, we'll go home, I'm fairly out of temper.'

The lady's temper remained uncertain for the rest of the day. Her reading of evening prayers was unwontedly short and sharp, and Jacquette was dismissed to bed early, at the same time as the servants.

The moon was almost full. It would befriend her that night, as it had done on the night of her escape from the castle. She opened her casement window and let in the sweet scents of the garden and the sea, that lay like a silver shield. Very softly Jacquette sang:

> 'Who gives this maid?' said Little John;
> Quoth Robin 'That do I!
> And he that takes her from Alan-a-Dale,
> Full dearly he shall her buy.'

V
May Madness

The chapel on the cliffs had been deserted since Margaretta Brandon had taken Jacquette and Father Robert away from it. In the moonlight it looked as forlorn as an abandoned nest, cold and stark. The hermit's presence had given it some protection, but now much of the stained glass had gone, filched by someone skilful at the top of a ladder, to make his own windows grand.

Alan was perched on a heap of stones, playing very softly on a flageolet. At sight of Jacquette he rose and came to meet her. In the fitful silver light she fancied an unearthly look about him, as though a young goat-god from the old times had come back to his ancient haunts. Now that he wore no cap she could see that his ears were very slightly pointed, and his eyebrows slanted upwards at the outer corners.

'Well met, mistress. So you made your escape?'

'As you see. Old Dame Annet's bedchamber is on one side of mine, and Mistress Brandon's on the other, but they both snore like dragons, and I have a light foot.'

He waved her to the stone-heap seat. 'Now I shall hear why I'm honoured by this meeting. I can guess before you tell me – I'm to be scolded for my clumsy cartomancy. Is that not it?'

'A little. I thought you not subtle enough with the cards. You should mystify the customer more, show other cards besides the three you turned up, and use a dark strange voice when you tell the fortune. That was my father's way, and he got great fame by it.'

Alan was smiling. 'Is that the whole of my fault?'

'No. Your reading of the cards was not as I know it. They like to hear of rich handsome strangers coming into their lives, and pots of gold and wonderful turns of luck. You gave me none of that – *and* you spoke of death. That you must never, never do, or you fright them out of their wits and they tell their neighbours, so that you lose your custom. You even frightened me a little, do you know!'

'But I saw death,' Alan answered seriously.

Jacquette drew back from him. 'You saw? How?'

'With the eyes of my mind. As I see clearly, sometimes.'

'But . . . That is divination, not fortune-telling. We make no use of that. My father knew the great Michel de Nostredame of Montpelier, and he used no such tricks, nor should you.'

'But it is not a trick. I have the gift of inner sight, and I can sometimes see the future plain.'

Jacquette regarded him gravely. 'Then you must not use it, or you'll be taken for a warlock, and what will become of you then? Promise, vow to me you'll put it aside.'

'How can I, mistress? I could no more shut off that power than you could help seeing a haystack by daylight. All I can promise is that I'll never speak of what I see.'

A question had been troubling her. 'When you saw death, was it mine?'

'No, mistress. I could not see whose it was.'

'Good. Because I would rather grow rich a better way. That is why I am here. Alan-a-Dale, I must go back to my trade! How can I settle to live all my life as I do now, shut up in weary dullness until I'm old and withered?'

'You have a roof over your head, and food and warmth.'

'I never slept roofless, when I travelled with my father. And Mistress Brandon keeps me as close as a gaoled thief – I may not do this, I may not do that, I am not to practise my skills or pass the time with anything but weary needlework, and making sweet lotions and washballs. I swear I often yawn more times in one day than I speak words.'

'You have a young gentleman to give you his protection in marriage. I saw how jealously he eyed you, and how he bore you off.'

'A dullard, a stuffed ape! I should yawn myself distracted after a day in his company.'

Alan regarded her quizzically. 'And you never thought of this till now? Come, mistress.'

'I thought him a clod, always. But no – only when I saw you at the fair, that was when I knew I must be free again.'

'My bad performance drew you so strongly?'

'No, it was not that. It was . . .' It was the look of him, his gestures, the way he spoke, an enchantment he had put upon her, unknowingly, as though he had wound a chain about her. Her face, turned up to his, was a dark flower, soft pools of shadow and pearly flesh, gleaming eyes and velvet mouth. 'Take me with you. Oh, take me with you!'

'I cannot, mistress. It would be a sin to take you from safety into peril. What do you know of English roads and the ways of the English with strolling folk?'

'I know them not very different from French roads and French ways!' she flashed back. 'My father and I entertained at inns and humble houses and great ones – even the King himself at his Court – though that ended not well,' she added, laughing at the memory of the purple royal face. 'So you see, I know all about it – I could perhaps tell *you* many things.'

Alan sighed. 'All this may be true. But it would never do for you, a maid, to travel the roads alone with a man who is no kin to you. Your good name would be gone.'

'But we would be married. Do you take me for a light maid?'

'*Married?* Mistress, are you out of your mind?'

'Oh! then you are – you have a wife already. Why did you not tell me, why did you let me talk so much?' Tears of disappointment had sprung to her eyes, glittering in the moonlight. Alan gently wiped them away as they fell.

'No, rest easy, I have no wife. There was a woman – but I am not bound to her. She never asked for marriage, or vows. Let go of my hand, for I must beg you to think of one more thing. This lady, the one who was with you at the fair and was not pleased to see you talk to me – is she kin to you?'

'She is my guardian. She took me away from here when I was living with Father Robert – you need not look so, we were sharing this old chapel as a refuge – and brought me up in her home, by St Margaret's church. She is Mistress Margaretta Brandon, a widow and a good sort of woman.'

'Then you owe her much gratitude for her charity. Could you leave her so unkindly, then, poor lady? I should not have thought you unkind.'

Jacquette was not unkind, and she had been brought up to

respect the rules of chivalry. She was not cruel either, only as unimaginative as all young creatures. A kitten, leaping to catch a butterfly, cares nothing for the creature's feelings nor pauses to wonder whether it has any; to Jacquette Mistress Brandon was a strong, all-powerful personage without weaknesses. One could not be kind or unkind to her, only dutiful or disobedient. Never having known her own mother, used only to an indulgent father's control, she had chafed at her guardian's discipline more than many girls would have done. She said:

'She will be angry, yes, for a time. She and Master Tuke will put their heads together and call me too bad to burn. But then she will forget, and find some other child to rear. Besides, I have to live my life, not hers. Never mind her. You *will* take me? It must be you and I – you and I!'

Alan was unconvinced and unhappy. He had meandered along very comfortably for years, drifting in and out of other strollers' company, aware that he was not the performer his father had been, nor as fond of showing off as the mummers he sometimes worked with, cavorting and clowning for laughs, the louder the better. He was charmed by the maid, allured as one might be by a beautiful many-hued bird, and he saw that she could teach him much. And yet his heart misgave him.

He turned away from the lovely pleading face and the warm hand on his arm. Near to where they sat a little pool had formed in the uneven ground, holding recent rain. In its still surface stars were reflected, and the gibbous moon, almost full. Suddenly the moon went behind a cloud, and only a dark glimmer remained. In it Alan saw with the eyes of his mind a clear picture: himself and Jacquette, in clothing strange to him, together in a place he did not recognise. He knew it for a vision of their inevitable future.

'I will take you,' he said abruptly. 'Go home now, and if you're still of the same mind meet me at first light the day after tomorrow. You know St Austin's Cross? There's a dingle close by where some of us gather. Say nothing more, but go.'

After the flitting figure was out of sight he tried to open the door of the chapel. It was open, there he spent the night, sometimes kneeling, sometimes sitting, watching the shapes in the high altarpiece come and go by the fitful light of the moon, praying (though he was no more pious than the next man) for a blessing on the path he would take with Jacquette Valencey.

For all her brave words, Jacquette went about nervously on what was to be her last day in the household, as though her guardian's sharp eyes might suddenly read of her coming flight in her face. Every summons made her start – and there were many, since her unruly behaviour at the fair had made Mistress Brandon suspicious that her charge was growing restive. It was often the case with maids in the month of May, and with all young things, but it must not be allowed to put the Lammas Day wedding in danger.

Which was why it seemed desirable to have another fitting of the wedding-dress. The sewing-maid, Mall, was summoned. Once again Jacquette was helped into the heavy farthingale, its velvet glowing like a newly-picked peach, to stand impatiently while Mall crawled round the great circle of it.

' 'Tis but a nip-fit here, mistress,' she said, ruefully displaying strained stitches.

'What!' Mistress Brandon cried. 'Swelling at the waist already, girl? We'll have none of that for six months yet, if you please.' Jacquette smiled dutifully, enduring the pulls and pats, the forcing of her unwilling flesh into the iron-stiffened Spanish body, and the painful dig of the stomacher's point, knowing she would never have to bear it again, though Mall's thick fingers, attaching the sleeves with pins, drew uncontrollable squeals as the pins found neck and bosom instead of cloth.

At last it was done, and she stood in the loosely held-together likeness of the finished gown. 'There.' Mall took the last of the pins out of her mouth. 'Is that not a picture?'

Mistress Brandon was gazing, her eyes unusually tender and her mouth soft. 'A picture indeed. I shall be proud of you on your bridal day, child.' She took off a long chain of interlinked gold and small pearls, on which hung a delicate ivory cross, and placed it round Jacquette's neck, saying, 'It graces you better than me.' It was a thing she always wore, given to her long ago by her mother. Jacquette felt a lump rise in her throat; for the first time she half-realised what she might be doing by deserting the woman who had given her so much. She knew nothing of the dead and miscarried infants, only sensed that there was something she had not understood or troubled to find out. Kissing Margaretta on both cheeks, she murmured ashamed thanks. At that moment she could have renounced her coming adventure; but it was too late, and the magic too strong.

It would be too cruel to take the neck-chain, or any of the small jewellery that had been birthday gifts. In a way it would be wrong to take anything, for surely that was a kind of theft. But one could not go naked. Some things she had that were her own.

When the Valenceys had left London to return to France, they had left behind in London a small coffer of conjuring apparatus and clothes, to be sent after them to Paris. Because Jacquette had lamented the loss of them, Mistress Brandon had made enquiries, written letters, and at last, after more than a year, had got the coffer back. It had, most fortunately, never been despatched to Paris. Amazingly, the lock was unbroken and nothing had been stolen. Jacquette had kept it carefully, a relic of her old life and of Estienne, and the only possession that was all hers, apart from the silver spoon, the dagger, and the wooden angel that had been in her pouch at Dover.

She knelt before the open coffer. The garments she had once worn were laughably small now, none of them wearable. But there were some clothes of Estienne's that he had thought too good for the journey to France: a velvet jerkin with silver buttons, a pair of embroidered sleeves, a ruffled shirt, a cap with ribbon falling-bands, a pair of worn but good hose. These would do for Alan, who was much of a size with Estienne.

There were other useful objects. Two packs of marked cards, dice and a throwing-cup, a little globe of the heavens with the stars shown in silver, a small, prettily-chased fipple-flute, and a jester's head in cap and bells at the end of a stick. Jacquette sat back on her heels, smiling. Such an ancient thing, perhaps made a hundred years ago, given to Estienne by an old, old jester. 'This is Loys,' he had said. 'When he laughs, your turn will go well. Keep his face clean and his bells bright.' Alas, poor Loys's face was grimy and his bells tarnished; but that would be remedied.

Folding the jerkin to get it into a small space, Jacquette's fingers found a curious stiffness and heaviness in its edge, under the braiding. There were rough stitches in the lining, stitches made by no woman's hand. Carefully she picked at them with a needle, until a shining thing began to emerge, a coin, a gold angel, so bright that it might have been newly minted. Beside it she could feel another – six or seven, perhaps more. A little fortune! Estienne must have prudently sewn them into the jerkin before they left London, and thought it safer to leave them behind than to carry them. He would be glad to see his daughter find them now.

These things, wrapped small in a meal-sack from an outhouse, were all the luggage Jacquette took with her. She wore her oldest kirtle, one she had almost grown out of, but its shortness would be an advantage, and her other garments were equally old and plain. She hesitated to take the good camlet cloak that had been new in the winter, but a cloak of some kind she must have. All her ornaments were laid out carefully on a table; it was a wrench to part with the coral and gold earrings. After some hesitation, she kept the ivory cross. It had been so kindly given, and might afford her some protection. Last of all, she sat down with pen, ink and paper to write what she must write; yet how to say it? 'Good Madam: you will be angry when you find me gone yet I cannot but go since I have met with one who shall be both husband and companion to me. I beg your forgiveness and thank you humbly for your great kindnesses. I trust another may fill my place better than I.'

It was poor, it was clumsy, but it would have to do.

That night, after prayers, Mistress Brandon bade her goodnight more lingeringly than usual.

'Your cheeks are on fire. I hope you have not caught a fever, junketing at the fair.'

'No, no, I am quite well. Goodnight, Madam.'

Then Margaretta Brandon said something that Jacquette would remember all her life. 'Goodnight, daughter.'

The first dawn-light was dappling the skies, the first cock crowing, when Margaretta Brandon awoke from uneasy, tossing sleep. Something had troubled her all the previous day, even when she proudly viewed Jacquette in the pinned-together wedding-gown. She was not a woman given to idle fancies, but she had suffered much in her life, and all too often an apprehensive fear had visited her: before she had lain down in childbed, to bear only a dead infant, or when a seemingly healthy one fell into a fever that would carry it out of her arms and into its grave. Something of the same cold foreboding had been on her, was still on her, as she put on her bed-gown and went from her bedchamber to Jacquette's.

None of the servants was stirring yet. Old Annet's rasping snores were audible still, but from Jacquette's room there was no sound. Margaretta pulled the latch and went in.

A look told her all, even before she picked up the letter in Jacquette's bold handwriting, with its postscript hastily added under the signature: 'I pray you do not search for me.' Margaretta laid the letter down. No, she would not search. News travelled slowly, messengers would be useless without a direction known. By now the girl might be on the high road to London or on the Channel bound for France, more likely. Another child had indeed been lost, and none, in spite of that wounding, thoughtless sentence, should ever fill her place.

St Austin's Cross was a battered stone monument with little shape left to it. A few hundred yards away was a hazel-wood, and not far within was a dell, a natural treeless hollow that was by tradition a resting-place for travellers.

They had been resting there that night, travellers of all sorts. On the far side tents were pitched, in and out of which moved true 'Egyptians', Romanies, the wandering folk whose origins were lost in time. Perhaps their ancestors had indeed come from Egypt, perhaps not. Two centuries earlier they had been in the East in great numbers, until the Tartar Emperor Tamburlaine let loose his forces on them and drove them out, to travel westward into Europe, where they were heartily disliked and dealt with severely.

Yet here they still were, in an English wood, strange figures in tattered cloaks, under which finer garments were hidden, filched from washing-lines or river banks where careless women had left them to dry. They moved with a tinkle of bells, which were sewn about them like Morrisers' bells, worn to attract an audience as they entered villages, dancing and beating tambourines. Scarves of many colours were tied round their heads, and their women wore great brass earrings, bracelets and girdles. Shabby nags grazed alongside the tents, mongrel dogs and half-naked children roamed the camp, among fires which were dying down now that the morning light was growing. Jacquette was glad that the tents were on the far side of the dingle, so that she did not have to pass among them. Suspicious dark eyes shot glances at her as she approached, but in her drab clothing, with a meal-sack for luggage, she looked not worth the plundering. If only they had known, she thought.

Down in the hollow, well removed from the Egyptian camp, were other travellers, many still sleeping, rolled in blankets. They were content enough to herd together in suitable places such as this, though very different in kind; *didekeis*, half-breed gypsies not accepted by the true ones, pedlars, wandering tinkers, and strolling entertainers. Jacquette recognised in a fat man the Friar Tuck of the Robin Hood performance, and a slatternly girl who was sitting up combing her hair as the Marian. Near them, tending something over a fire, was Alan.

He was startled to see her, and showed it. All her wild talk might have been only moon-madness, to be forgotten in the light of day. Yet here she was, dressed most plainly, not tricked out in finery, as she might well have been, sturdy and confident as though she had been a traveller all her life. But then she had, for much of it.

Curious eyes were fixed on her, as she approached. The girl who played Marian stopped combing, and stared, as Alan took the newcomer's hands, hostility in her gaze.

Alan said, 'I thought you would not come.'

'Then you don't know me. Look what I brought –' As she was about to open the sack Alan stopped her.

'Not here. Too many watchers.'

'Oh. But you'll be pleased when you see. Have I dressed well? Do I look like one of these?'

'Not foul enough, but it will do.' The girl watching them uncoiled herself and strolled across. She was taller than Jacquette remembered, thin, long-limbed with a dancer's muscular legs. Without paint her face was pale and spotty, and none too clean. Her long brown hair fell about her like a cloak, lending her a certain grace. Her eyes raked Jacquette from head to foot, pausing enviously on her healthy complexion and smooth hands. There had been a woman, Alan had told Jacquette, and this was she.

'So, a fine lady's come to visit the poor?' she mocked. 'How did your ladyship leave the Court, then, and aren't them noble lords all amort at missing you? Come to hand out some charity, eh?' She made a grab at the sack, which Alan foiled, seizing her wrist and flinging her off.

'Leave that, Grizel,' he said shortly. 'This is Jacquette, a friend I met with lately. She follows our trade.'

'Oho, does she, then? As a mort, or a bawdy-basket, or a glimmer-hunter?'

'None, mistress.' Jacquette understood very well the language of the roads and the distinctive terms for strolling females, 'I'm no beggar, I'd have you know, but an honest maid and daughter to a notable *jongleur*.'

'What cant's that, jongler? And what name did our Alan give you – Jacket, was it? Or Jacko – that's the ape's name.' Her hands were tensing for the attack with nails on a rival's face that was the common way of warfare among her kind. Alan, seeing it, thrust her forcefully off, so that she staggered and cursed. Friar Tuck laughed fatly, applauding. Alan went over to a recumbent figure half-hidden beneath a bush, shook it and shouted, 'Wake, Father! your services are called on. Look sharp, now.'

The bundle stirred, groaned, yawned, and emerged slowly from its wrappings, to reveal itself as an elderly man of frowsty appearance, with a grey straggling beard and a thin fringe of grey hair around a tonsure. Getting to his feet, he sketched the sign of the cross in Alan's direction. He was a hedge-priest, one of those who might or might not have been in Holy Orders but who now lived by solemnising marriages between wandering folk, giving couples who wished it a semblance of respectability. All handfastings before witnesses were legal, but the presence of a priest made them even more binding, even though the garbled ceremony was not according to the liturgy of the new Protestant Church.

'This is our *patrico*, Father Jerome,' Alan said. 'Father, greet

Mistress Jacquette Valencey. You are to bless our handfasting, if you will. Come, I did tell you of this last night.'

'Oh . . . ah . . . very true, my son. Good morrow to your sweet lady.' Suppressing an immense yawn, he stumbled towards them. 'Give me your hand, son Alan, and yours, mistress.' His own grimy one enclosed them, and he muttered, '*Ego vos conjungo in matrimonio* . . .' If he had ever been familiar with the old-style marriage ceremony most of it had slipped from his mind, but the dog-Latin served well enough for most of his customers. At last he came to '*In nomine Patris, et Filii, et Spiritu Sancti, Amen.*'

Alan kept Jacquette's hand in his own. His eyes held hers as he said gravely, 'I take thee, Jacquette, for my wife.'

'I take thee, Alan, for my husband,' she answered. Again the old man blessed them, then eagerly extended his claw for a fee. Jacquette, in a kind of daze, watched him go back to his place beneath the bush, delightedly counting the pence. Of all strange marriages, this must be the strangest. She had told Alan they must be married, yet had never thought of how it would come about: this garbled ceremony in the open, a hedge-priest for clergyman, vagrants for a congregation, and for husband a man she had spoken with only three times. Was it madness, or magic, the lure that had drawn her to him at first sight, the beckoning that had bewitched her out of home, and safety, and a Christian marriage?

Alan drew her towards him and kissed her on the mouth. And that was truly magic, for suddenly she was not troubled any more, but smiled at him like any bride, feeling a warm glow of excited happiness. The grey light of early morning changed into the rosy gold of first sunlight, glinting down on them through the lacework of the trees as though they stood beneath a great window of stained glass.

'Come, wife,' he said. 'We must be on our way. Today we dine at Canterbury.'

VI
Bridebed at The Chequers

Dinner-time was long past when they reached Canterbury, having talked so much on the road that their pace had been slower than they intended. Jacquette told Alan her story, and learned from him things there had been no time to ask before. He was nineteen, and had been born and reared in a great house in Wiltshire – which explained why he spoke so like a gentleman, but with an accent strange to Kentish ears. His grandfather had been resident entertainer to the lord of the manor, one who loved laughter and song, and the post had descended to his son. But when the old lord died things changed at the manor; the new heir had little love for entertaining, and Alan's father and mother became hardly more than servants on the pay-roll with nothing to do but amuse guests at rare feast-times.

The boy had grown up in loneliness, the only survivor of young sisters and brothers who died in a plague outbreak, trained to no trade, picking up from his parents the physical skills, acrobatics and dancing, some tricks of sleight of hand, the way to deceive with cards and dice, and the use of his own talent for music. When the parents too died, of the lung-sickness one hard winter, Alan had gone out into the world armed only with these few skills, and had found it a hard world indeed. Taken up by the strolling mummers, who went about performing the Mask of Robin Hood and other country entertainments, he learned much about the ways of the road – and of other matters from Grizel the dancer.

He had been born with his other skill, for sometimes seeing the future, and things not visible to the eye. Jacquette should know no more of it than she need. She had spoken sharply about it, and he would try to keep from annoying her again.

The gilded six-winged angel on the cathedral tower glittered in the afternoon sun as they came into the city. Alan had visited it, but very briefly, as Fat Matt, the Tuck of the party, had got into a brawl at the alehouse where they stayed, and the others had left hastily before they were all arrested. He was all eyes for the fine houses and shops and churches, but Jacquette propelled him past them.

'I'm hungry, starving – never mind all this, it will wait, we can see it later.'

'But where are we going?'

'To an inn.'

With unsavoury memories of the alehouse, the communal bed the lodgers had shared on the floor, and the still more unsavoury charms of the resident whore, Black Bess, Alan was amazed to be halted in the High Street before a splendid house of ancient timbers, its broad eaves overhanging the street, at the corner of the little lane leading to the cathedral.

'You surely don't mean to stay here, mistress . . . wife?'

'Make up your mind, for I'll not be mistress-ed now. And why should we not stay here? *I* have stayed here before, and my father. Have you not heard of the Chequers of the Hope, the pilgrims' hostel since St Thomas's time, the most famous inn of Canterbury?'

'But we are not pilgrims,' Alan pointed out.

'Of course not – nor is anyone else, since old King Henry stole the Shrine and banished the monks. Follow me.' With a serene authority which she had assumed with the estate of wifehood, Jacquette swept through the long courtyard, ignoring the glances of ostlers and inn-servants, and through the door of a parlour where a girl was strewing clean rushes.

'Fetch me the landlord,' she ordered.

Alan was not surprised that the landlord, a corpulent man with sharp eyes and a tight mouth, viewed them with extreme suspicion and told them plain, 'I don't want your sort here. Be gone.'

Jacquette outfaced him. 'I think you do, landlord. We may look like tattercoats, but looks are often liars, as they say. My good man and I travelled here in this plain guise because we feared robbers, having been warned they were about. Is that not so, husband?'

'True,' said Alan, trying to keep up with her. 'Very fierce villains. Armed,' he added as a convincing touch.

'A good story.' The landlord's smile was mirthless. 'And a very old one.' He was impressed with their superior speech, but that was a trifle. 'I might believe it better if I saw the colour of your money, mistress.'

Alan, conscious of the few poor pence in his pouch, prepared to leave, but Jacquette said lightly, 'A fine colour, to my thinking.' She opened her hand: in the palm lay a gold angel.

Both men stared at it, Alan hardly believing his eyes.

'It's good, sound,' Jacquette said, biting it in proof. 'Will it pay for a lodging tonight? When I lodged here with my father, God rest his soul, five years ago take or leave, we lay in a little chamber beyond the Dormitory of the Hundred Beds – I should like that, if you have it free.'

'Aye, mistress. My best.' Wiping his hands on his apron, he led them with a show of obsequiousness up an outside stair into the upper storey of the inn, through a long, spacious room with a high-pitched raftered roof supported by pillars. It was, Jacquette told Alan, the place where the mass of the pilgrims had slept in old days, tired from their long journeys. Here they talked, jested, and told tales, and at break of day went joyfully out by a little stairway to the roof, to view the great bulk of the cathedral's west side below them. 'Now they are scattered, like the jewels of the Shrine, and only the common run of travellers stay.'

'More's the pity,' muttered the landlord. He showed them into a small dark room adjoining, at the sight of which Jacquette gave a cry of delight. It was the same one she had occupied with Estienne; they had been very tired, and thought it luxury. It held a bed and little else but a stool and a very small chest; behind the bed hung a faded tapestry of the Fall of Man.

Jacquette thanked the landlord coolly, and dismissed him. Alan broke out, 'Where did you get that gold? It was not playing fair, not to tell me. I might have spoken and spoiled all.'

'If you think I stole it you are quite wrong, and I blush for you. It's mine, got honestly, and I'll show you how.' She began to unfasten the sack. Alan stopped her with a gesture, went to the door and opened it suddenly. Nobody was there, the dormitory empty.

Jacquette took out the contents of the sack, chattering excitedly. 'These were all my father's. See, they're a perfect fit for you! And all these were his, things we shall take on the road with us. And here, look, this is the source, the mine of gold . . .' She showed the slit in the jerkin and the lurking brightness within. 'I kept just one of them out, and lo, the metamorphosis in that mean fellow! Now, put on the jerkin and the hose –'

'First I must wash,' Alan said firmly. 'One should not don fine clothes when all of a muck-sweat.' Before he had finished speaking Jacquette was out of the room, down the stairs and into the yard. Returning, she nodded with satisfaction. 'They are bringing water.' Curiously she watched Alan untie his points and take off his hose and worn doublet. It was long since she had seen a man undress, and then it had been her father, but after all this one was her husband. His skin was very white and fine, below the brown throat; she thought he looked like the young St Sebastian, but for the arrows. Alan caught her gazing, and blushed. Her own colour deepened, and she gave him a smile of excited happiness.

Together they went out into the streets, Alan now to all appearances a respectable citizen escorting a humble wench. The wench, who had a nose for such things, found a booth where were sold garments ready made up, second-hand from other wearers. Jacquette examined them, sniffed them, tested the stitches, and then pronounced them clean and fit to wear, 'though I hope,' she said aside loudly to Alan, 'they may not have come from a house of plague.' The stall-keeper swore, with many sacred oaths, that they had not, and Jacquette bore away a pair of handsome slashed sleeves, an overkirtle, a pretty frontal of lace with a separate ruff which tied on, and a flat black cap of wool.

In their room at the Chequers she put on her new garments, all but the cap. Then she combed out her hair, plaited all the shining length of it, and wound the plaits round and round her head, where they formed a kind of flat wreath. 'Now I am a married woman,' she said, 'it is not fitting to wear my hair down. Besides, the cap sits on it so jimply.'

'But,' Alan pointed out, 'those who come to see us entertain expect to see flowing hair – that fashion is too sedate and formal.'

'Oh.' Jacquette was tilting her head this way and that, admiring the effect in the hand-mirror she had brought away with her. 'Did you see me buy the pins? I thought the woman sold them very cheap, six for a groat.' She came to him and took his hands in hers, her eyes laughing into his. 'Well, if you say so, my lord and master, I will wear my hair uncoiffed on the road. Like this I am your grave, serious wife – like that I shall be your merry maid.'

'That is what they call female strollers,' Alan said, 'merrymaids – as we are merrymen. It suits you well, pretty wife.' He did indeed begin to wonder if his life had not been a very dull thing until this remarkable young woman came into it.

'Strange,' Jacquette reflected. 'Once I was taken for a mermaid, and nearly got my death by it. Now I am a merrymaid I hope for a better fate.'

'Your fate at this moment is the best supper Canterbury can provide,' Alan said. They went out into the street, their arms entwined round each other's waist, and people smiled to see them.

They feasted on meat and spiced ale and strawberries from the tavern's garden, and went early to the wide bed in the small room, where they pleased each other wonderfully well: the bride who knew nothing of love and found it a delightful discovery, and the groom who had learnt it in a rough school, yet was himself most gentle. 'Blooming the fruit of Love's desire', said the song of the shepherd's love: and so bloomed Alan's love with her new wifehood. They slept at last in each other's arms, as soundly as children.

It was Alan who heard the faint furtive clinking sounds. He raised his head from the pillow, instantly awake. At first he could make out nothing in the darkness; then, against the small uncurtained window, a moving shape came and went. Jacquette's breathing was soft and regular, undisturbed. A suppressed curse came from the intruder, and a thud, as though he had stumbled. A fine thief to go robbing in the dark, thought Alan, and at that moment a great weight came down on him.

There was heavy cloth pressing his face into the pillow,

stopping his breath, imprisoning the edge of the counterpane so that he could not get his arms free. A choking cry from Jacquette told him that the weight was on her face, too. As she threshed about beside him he thought that if there were only one attacker, they had a chance of escape – if two, they were dead. Suddenly his flailing right arm found a gap, where the bedclothes had been dragged away from the side of the bed. He used it to grasp at the assailant, catching him by surprise. The man let go his pressure to fend off the hand; instantly Alan sat up, throwing off the blanket that had been smothering him, and grappled with the unseen enemy. Jacquette, released, gave a loud scream.

'Go for him! Scratch, do anything you can!' Alan cried, at the same time finding a throat and gripping it. Its owner, gasping, tried to pull away, but Alan, naked and slippery as an eel, was out of the bed and in control of the struggle.

A scraping sound and the flash of a spark told him that Jacquette had found the tinder-box on the stool at her side of the bed. A rush-light was by it. The next moment a flood of golden light filled the room, showing her the wrestling forms on the floor. She ran round the bed and lent her strength to the attack. The man groaned, giving up the struggle. As he rolled over they saw the face of the landlord.

He was a far bigger man than Alan, but his extra weight made him no match for one who was a trained acrobat, and in any case he was winded from his fall. He glared up at the two young naked creatures who were regarding him without favour.

'You took too much on yourself, friend,' Alan said, 'to rob two sleepers single-handed. Next time you'll know better. Now get up, and never think but I can master you again.' He glanced at the chest, where the conjuring devices, neatly laid out the night before, had been disarranged in the man's blind search for gold. 'You found little worth, I see – though this might very fitly reward you for your pains.' He jangled the fool's head mockingly. Jacquette laughed.

'Go back to your bed,' Alan ordered him, 'and nurse your bruises, and be thankful I haven't sent my wife for the constable.' The landlord shambled out; they heard him pass through the great dormitory and slam the door. Jacquette looked down at herself, then at Alan.

'Adam and Eve – and a Serpent who would have fanged them both.' She shivered, not from cold; Alan drew her to him. 'Eve was a gallant wench to find a light. But for that . . . love, we must go. He nodded at the dim tapestry. 'This chamber was Eden tonight, but tomorrow will see a change.'

'What will he do?'

'Something, to save his face – and it will not be asking whether we slept well, and serving us a hearty breakfast. My guess is that he'll send for a constable – plague take it, that I put that notion into his head! – and have us arrested on suspicion of carrying stolen gold.'

'But we would tell – accuse him . . .'

'We are not known in Canterbury, and he is, and if they searched us the gold would be found and his case proved. It would be unjust, but life is not always just. Let's dress, and be out of here before light.'

At the end of small Mercery Lane the great Christ Church gateway reared its battlemented head, its stone front splendid with gilding and the brilliant colours of many painted coats of arms, visible even in the semi-dark of the May night. The carved oaken doorway was shut. Jacquette breathed a prayer to St Thomas that his benign influence might follow them on their journey. And because it might bring them luck, she said to Alan that they must follow the Pilgrims' Way.

VII

Jacquette draws the Queen of Clubs

Now that they were decently clad and well equipped, it seemed only fitting that they should no longer tramp the roads. As Jacquette pointed out, hay costs no more than shoe-leather. Not far on their way, near the little town of Faversham, where it was market-day, a sale of horses was being held in a meadow by the roadside. Jacquette had had little to do with horse-flesh, but Alan had known and sometimes ridden the beautiful creatures kept by the lord of Norton Manor, his birthplace. None of the animals on sale could be said to be beautiful, but neither were they worn-out gypsy nags smartened up for selling, dosed with drugs, made from herbs, given to them to make them deceptively lively.

Alan's eye for a beast was better, but Jacquette was the sharper bargainer. For a sum she could well afford, she bought two geldings, a brown and a pied chestnut. Both were small, compactly-built, and seemingly of a good temper. Jacquette chose the chestnut, calling him Blaise because of the white blazon on his nose, while Alan named the brown one Ned, for the boy King.

Jacquette was nervous and uncertain of Blaise at first, by no means confident of staying on his back with the side-saddle they had to buy. But he trotted so amiably, and responded so well to blandishments and small treats, of which he had not had many in his short life, that she was soon reassured. It was a luxury to get rid of the meal-sack and carry their possessions in two bundles, one to each horse's back.

The time had come to plan and perfect the performances they would give. Some of the skills they shared, some were known to only one of them. Jacquette chose their rehearsal-place, beneath a flowering hawthorn-hedge in a field where there was none to see them, but for a boy herding geese, who cast a dull eye over them, then lost interest. Jacquette spread their equipment out on the short daisy-spangled grass. They had bought more on the journey; a half-dozen coloured kerchiefs, a string of bright wooden beads, a bunch of laces, and some counters.

With these, and what they already had, they went through all the tricks most popular with spectators. This was a pleasant occupation for a May morning, since their hands often touched and it was necessary to sit very close together. Alan's hands were very beautiful, Jacquette thought, not as strong as her own but more elegant, like the hands of a nobleman. He found a great fascination in her trick of downward-looking, then suddenly raising her eyes to his so that he seemed to swim in their darkness, and it became necessary to stop their practising and kiss.

'When you secretly untie the knot in the handkerchief,' Jacquette said, 'you should do it with a charm, the better to impress them with your learning.'

'What charm – *Pax, Max, Fax?*'

'No, no, that's too simple. You must say – let me think – ah, yes. *Droch myroch, senaroth, betu baroch assmanoth, rousee farounsee, hey passe passe.*'

'They'll take that for devils' language.'

'Not they, and what if they do? Keep the other for throwing in if a trick goes slowly. Now the beads. We want three – so, and one must have a hole bigger than the rest. That's easily done with the point of a dagger. Now – two cords of two foot long each, that will give us four ends. Then we put that bead on the end . . .' The beads at first refused to stay where they were put, which caused some agreeable scuffling for them in the grass. Alan said that he would never master such a trick. Nor was he as smooth as she at pulling coloured laces out of his mouth in a continuous string, even talking through them, and both conjurors were overcome with laughter, attracting the attention of the goose-boy, who took them for dangerous wandering lunatics, and moved his flock further off.

'Let's turn to the cards,' said Alan. 'You spoke harshly to me of my prophecies at the fair.'

'That was because you used your own tricks of divination –

and I have seen no token of *that* these two days. Did you not "see" what that scoundrelly landlord would try on us?'

'Alas, no, sweetheart. There I failed you. The thing comes and goes, it is not constant.'

'Good – it can go and never come back, for me. Now: I shall write all this down for you, and a picture of each card against it, but listen first. For every one who consults you there is a different meaning,' she propounded solemnly. 'If a woman draws the Seven of Hearts, and she is a young wench, foretell her marriage, but for an old wife only pleasant company, unless she wears widow's weeds, and then you may predict a second wedding. If a woman draws the Queen of Clubs, she has a rival – if a man, he will have a strong supporter. The Five of Diamonds means for a man that he will thrive best at home, for a woman that she should travel for good luck. For the Ace, tread carefully; the man who draws him will find him a fierce hot love, the woman, a mate rich and witty.'

'I have drawn him again and again, and see, the prophecy was true,' Alan said, picking up his instructor's left hand and kissing it. She regarded it with horror, not for the kiss, but for the bareness of one finger.

'Alan, my ring! We never thought . . . they'll take me for your doxy. How can I go about like a *putain*? We must get one, buy one today, this very hour. Oh, but not a costly one, only a plain band to show me honest. Come, let's leave this and go now!'

In Sittingbourne town they found a jeweller with a good store of rings that were not too fine. Alan chose one with 'My Love is Trew' inscribed around the inside, and put it on her finger when they were some way from the shop, out of sight of anyone. 'None can slander you now, sweet love.'

Lord, Lord, he thought to himself as they walked back to their tethered horses, was such a pair of innocents ever seen walking the world? The courtship done in a day and a night, the marriage so soon after, and that made by a hedge-priest, a bride so free with her gold that our marriage-bed might well have been our deathbed too: a husband forgetting of the ring, poor lackwit, and a wife no better in memory. How shall we do, two babes in the wild wood, with rogues and cozeners on every side? Better if we had never met, never set out together.

These pretty babes, with hand in hand,
Went wandering up and down;
But never more could see the man
Approaching from the town . . .

And his spirits, usually so equable, were quite low.

But they began confidently enough on their first working day, after much rehearsal, trying out their entertainment in a village north-east of the London road, near the sea. Enquiries at the nearest inn had told them that no other players, mummers or minstrels had visited it lately. Approaching, they dismounted and Jacquette led the horses while Alan played a cheerful tune on the hurdy-gurdy. At the tiny village green they stopped, tethered their docile mounts where there was good grass, and set themselves up in the middle of the green – by the stocks, as it happened, but they were fortunately unoccupied. In his come-all-ye speech to any who would listen, Alan jested that if their performance were bad, the good people had his leave to set them in the stocks. A ripple of laughter came from those who had strayed out of their cottages. Soon there were ten assembled to listen to his music, then a few more; enough to make a collection at the end.

To charm the crowd, without asking too much of their wits, Jacquette danced. She chose a dance of her own country, a *Pavane*, stately and languorous, in a minor key. Then, to the soft accompaniment of Alan's drum, beating out the rhythm, she sang the words:

'"Belle qui tiens ma vie
Captive dans tes yeux,
Qui m'as l'âme ravie
D'un souris gracieux,
Viens tôt me secourir
Ou me faudra mourir." '

Then she curtsied, low and respectful, to those who had never been curtsied to before, a picture of prettiness, with her beaming wide smile and her hair flowing, bound back with a scarlet ribbon. The men fell in love with her, the women took note of everything she wore. Then, so that the hearers should not think the programme too foreign and therefore suspect, Alan sang, without accompaniment, the song of 'The Cuckoo's Nest', with many expressive gestures in case anybody failed to understand the words; which was unlikely.

> As I went out a-walking one morning in May,
> I met a fair maid and unto her did say:
> 'For love I am inclined, I'll tell to thee my mind,
> For I'm mightily beguiled with thy cuckoo's nest.'

One must have a little bawdry, a trifle of country matters, in a country entertainment. The hearers roared their approval and shouted for more, even those who cried, 'Fie for shame'.

It was time to dazzle them with conjuring, having softened them with music. Jacquette set out the table, with the cups and balls and the cards, and beckoned the watchers to come near, which they did, awed and excited, even the men, though they pretended to leave that sort of thing to women and girls. In their dull lives this was the peak and sum of entertainment.

By agreement, only those tricks were done which Alan knew well; it would not do to blunder, for word got about swiftly, even from such a remote place. To the accompaniment of 'Oohs' and 'Aahs' and cries of 'Did you ever?', the two ran through their repertoire of tricks that were simple but sensational: the egg walking up a stick, the coin passing through a handkerchief, the unblown egg vanishing before one's very eyes, then reappearing from a man's ear or the bosom of a shrieking girl. Among the cries of admiration there were some superstitious mutterings, some hasty self-crossings, for these were folk to whom witchcraft was real and fearful. Jacquette, used to more sophisticated spectators, noted them, and was wary. At the end of the performance she stepped forward and, with a ravishing smile, opened her arms as though to embrace them all.

'Good people, we thank you for your gracious charity,' she said loudly, one eye on Alan, who was collecting in a bonnet what she guessed would be very small coins indeed. 'If we pleased you we are heartily glad of it – if we frighted any of you, we are heartily sorry, for we use no spells, only common devices and sleight of hand. We are as good Christian folk as you, and mean no ill.'

With that she bowed, and turned away to assemble the equipment. The crowd hung about hopefully for a few minutes, then began to disperse raggedly.

Alan showed the takings, with a rueful look. 'Enough to buy a pot of ale apiece, no more.'

'I could have told you so. Much trouble for little reward. Look on it as preparation for better things.'

He shook his head. 'For me, I expect no more – but for you, so proficient, so dextrous, and the prettiest maid these yokels can have seen in a month of Sundays . . .'

'I waste my sweetness? No, husband, they can give little who have little, and there were some who gave nothing at all – doubtless because they had nothing. Be merry! We did well enough, for a beginning. The next time we shall have a triumph.'

But the next time, and the next and the next were strangely disappointing. The money was scanty, the response of the audience not what Jacquette had expected and hoped for. Her dancing and singing drew applause, but it was loudest when the song was lively and the steps showed her ankles. Neither grace nor wit held them for long; what they wanted was laughter. Lewd jests and bawdy songs were meat and drink to them, women as much as men. Again and again they would shout for the ballad of 'The Rambling Tinker', with its broad double meanings which fooled nobody, and others of its kind – tales of country copulation, cuckolded husbands and wanton wives, lustful friars and ready-ripe maids. Alan knew such songs and could sing them with sly effect, but though no Puritan he was not at ease in them, being a modest youth more given to dreams and fancies than to bawdry. His audience could divine this very well, and gave him the less applause for it.

Jacquette found such stuff easier to perform, being more of a professional than Alan. But she was irked that two such young and personable creatures as they were could not make a good living out of material that was delicate and fine. Even the naughty French ditties which had amused Margaretta Brandon had been lightly witty, not designed for clowns to guffaw at. 'Oh, to be in London!' she sighed. 'There they have a good ear and good taste. Shall we go there, love, soon? My father had friends at Court, that knew me as a child. *They* would value us, *they* would not expect us to be always *licencieux*.'

But Alan said that they must work their way to London, earning as they went. The little store of gold angels had shrunk, with the buying of their clothes, and the horses, and the cost of lodging and stabling. To spend them all would be to leave nothing over for a rainy day, said prudent Alan; there might come a time when one or both of them could not work. Better to bear with sparse takings and arrive in London solvent, with their skills polished to perfection. They were as happy as any two could be, in this fine dry summer, by each other's side all day, sleeping by night in mean rooms on narrow beds. Jacquette prayed that she would not find herself with child too soon, and in this heaven was kind to her.

Because they were travelling fast London-wards, and thought it best to remain in the country for the summer months, they turned outwards across Kent and over the Surrey boundary, still following the Pilgrims' Way. Subtly the landscape changed, fields and farms having almost a foreign look to the travellers – thickly tree-clad hillsides and ferny commons, sparse hamlets, and a sense of the sea growing more and more distant. Taking too sharp a turn south, they lost their way, and travelled for many miles without knowing where they were, since such natives as they encountered were singularly ignorant of any place-name but their own, and suspicious of strangers so oddly dressed. They were in mid-county, tired and dust-caked with slogging up hills, walking the horses, and riding down them into country still unknown, when, thankfully circling a great wooded hill, they came down into a valley. A pretty river ran here and they followed its windings to a considerable town, which they learnt, was Dorking.

At least they were certain of a good night's lodging in a respectable inn, after a number of dismal alehouses and occasional nights in the open. They rode down the busy High Street, scanning the many inn-signs for the most likely one. Suddenly Alan exclaimed, 'You're hurt! What is it? Why didn't you tell me?' and pulled up Ned to stare at her.

'Hurt? No. What do you mean?'

'Your brow – a great wound. Stop, let me see it.' But as she reined in Blaise, Alan said wonderingly, 'It's vanished – gone!'

Jacquette put her hand to her smooth brow. 'There is nothing – I have no hurt. You were mistaken, love – it was a trick of shadows, or sunlight.'

'Yes, so it must have been. Yet . . .' He had seen it clearly, the raw edges of the wound, the blood on her eyelid and cheek.

At their chosen inn, the White Hart, they learnt that a great number of people were expected in the town early next morning, for it was Midsummer Day and there was to be a great fair held, with market-stalls, entertainments, and all kinds of revel. They had arrived at the perfect time, then, Jacquette said; they would be rested and ready by first light.

The day was as fine as they could have hoped, the crowd large. For all the heat there was ox-roasting and pig-roasting, fire-eaters swallowing hot coals, dancing and fiddling and sports. Alan and Jacquette had wisely left the horses stabled at the inn, for on such a day there were thieves about. They chose a pitch on the edge of the activities and stayed there, confining their act to conjuring and fortune-telling. Folk were generous; by late afternoon they had made more than in all the previous week. That evening they supped well at their inn. Alan, succumbing to tiredness and the unaccustomed wine they had drunk, went early to bed, but Jacquette had enough energy left to go to see to the horses before joining him.

'They have not been ridden all day, poor beasts. I have no trust in ostlers at such a large inn, either to feed them or bed them properly.'

The sun had gone down in heavy clouds after that beautiful day, and the stable-yard was a place of dusk and shadows, no sounds but the faint neighings and rustlings of the horses. Whoever had been looking after them by day was now sleeping or drinking indoors. Jacquette approached the stall where they were stabled together, calling their names, to be answered by pleased whinnying. She caressed their noses, talked to Blaise and Ned softly, gave each a nibble of fruit kept from the supper-table. It was good to have such gentle companions, who bore one's weight all day with little reward, yet felt no malice, only gratitude for a kind word and a pat on their soft muzzles. '*Mes amis, mes camarades, dormez doucement . . .*'

An arm came round Jacquette's throat from behind, compressing it in an agonising grip, while another arm encircled her body and swung her round with such force that her head banged against the wood of the stall. Frightened, the horses neighed and backed. The attacker's face was close to hers, spitting out words like bullets.

'French whore. Filthy French trull. Daggle-tailed man-stealer. Foul sneakin' blowen.' With every word Jacquette's head was jerked back viciously. She knew, through the pain and dizziness, that the woman was Grizel, the Marian of the Robin Hood Mask.

'I been doggin' you,' went on the voice, 'day and night, since you filched my *chy*. Everywhere you been I follered, French whore. I seen you at the fair today but you never seen me, eh? Now I got you safe.' The abuse came steadily, low-toned, hate-filled, the cant of the gutter mixed with Romany words. The woman was as strong as a man and as cunning as a wrestler in knowing where pain would be felt most.

Releasing her victim for a second, she stepped back and delivered a savage kick to one of Jacquette's shins, at the same time brandishing a knife. It came down just as Jacquette fainted with pain, falling so heavily against the half-door of the horses' stall that it gave way and took her with it.

Thus she never felt the knife-blow that missed her throat, but gashed her forehead from hair-line to eye. The scream she did not hear herself brought voices, footsteps and lights. When they reached her she lay motionless among the straw, almost under the hooves of the terrified horses. Of Grizel there was no sign.

VIII
A Charm too many

Jacquette was on the pallet-bed where she and Alan had slept the night before, a sheet crumpled under her head to catch the blood that was pouring from it. She was dizzy and faint with the pain of the knife-wound and a duller pain just above one temple, where she had hit her head on the stone floor when she fell. Alan was leaning over her, his face streaked with tears, calling her name over and over, and there were others behind him, peering down at her and talking. Then someone was bathing the wound, washing the blood away and hissing with dismay at the depth of the cut. She tried to say that they should do something about the leg that had been kicked, but no words would come out. Seeming all one pain, she fainted again.

When she came to, a bandage had been wound round her head, which was slightly raised on a cushion. Alan sat beside her; they were alone. As if from a distance, she heard him speaking to her. 'Better,' she whispered, and managed a smile. He held something to her mouth.

'Drink if you can, my love.' It was aqua-vitae, a powerful spirit, burning and glowing its way down, the sharp fumes rising to the brain, helping to clear it. When he withdrew the cup she signed for more, and he let her drink, knowing that it would lessen the pain. After a moment she pushed it away and lay back. Alan took her hand, holding it in both of his. She had never seen him, or anyone, look more ravaged.

'Who was it?' he asked gently. 'What fiend could have done such a thing to you?'

'Not fiend, friend.' She was surprised to find how much it hurt to speak: that arm had been round her throat like a vice. 'Your – comrade – of the greenwood.'

'Who? Not Tom – or Matt?'

'Marian.' The real name eluded her. 'She – followed me. Hates me. Jealous.'

'Grizel! that hellcat? *She* did this to you? I can't believe . . .' Yet he could believe it, remembering himself, an all too innocent boy, getting into the company of those three on the road. The men were honest enough in matters of friendship; the woman, Tom's doxy at the time, experienced and insatiably greedy for men, fell upon the tender green he-virgin and taught him her own knowledge, good and bad. He had sensed the bad part of it, had known that she was bad, yet her overpowering sexuality had had a fascination he was too raw to resist. She half-admired his gentle speech and courteous ways, yet despised them too, for she herself was of the tinker blood, with only a drop of true Romany in it. Alan had broken away from her and adventured in other fields, yet Fortune seemed to bring them together again significantly often. Because he had never formed a strong attachment to another woman until Jacquette, Grizel had thought herself sure of him, even let herself be a little fond of him, the most clean and courtly lover she had ever known.

And so she had planned Jacquette's murder.

'By Christ's Holy Blood, I shall see her hanged,' said Alan.

'No,' Jacquette croaked. 'It is ugly, to hang women. And I – am not dead, you see, because she missed –' she gestured towards her throat, where dark bruises were showing. 'I shall not die. But . . .' tears filled her eyes and began to course down her cheeks. 'Oh Alan, my face is spoiled! I can never be a *jongleuse* again.'

'You can, you will. I swear it, sweetheart.'

Early in the morning he sought out a physician, one recommended by the landlord. The old man was not best pleased to be fetched out before the sun was well up, or to be made to climb one of the White Hart's twisting staircases, but he had been shown a piece of money which lent speed to his arthritic steps. His boy at his heels, he entered stooping into the low-ceilinged room, and peered critically at his patient, who, with her white face half-obscured by a bloody bandage, could have passed for a casualty retrieved from the battlefield.

'Tush, tush,' said Doctor Piper, seizing her hand and examining it knowledgeably. 'You have a running fever, young madam.'

'No, indeed, sir.'

'Then you soon would have, had I not been summoned.' He snapped his fingers for the boy, who advanced with a silver bleeding-bowl and a lancet in a case, which the doctor flourished professionally before pushing up Jacquette's sleeve to find a vein. Alan intervened.

'She has lost so much blood already – would you rob her of more?'

Doctor Piper favoured him with a stern glare. 'Do you know what you say, young man? Bleeding lets out the ill humours, cools the brain, dispels poisons and strengthens the heart. Of course she must be bled.'

'I would rather not be.' Jacquette was emboldened by Alan's protest. 'I am very cool – feel my cheek – and there is no poison, or I would know it.'

'And the blood has stopped flowing,' Alan put in eagerly. 'I staunched it with a very good charm, invoking Our Lord. It began to lessen as soon as I spoke it – isn't that true, wife?'

The doctor's small spectacles were glinting from one to the other of them. 'Charm? What charm?' he barked.

'Why, this.' And the innocent Alan recited:

'Sanguis mane in te, sicut fecit Christus in se;
Sanguis mane in tua vena, sicut Christus in sua poena;
Sanguis mane fixus, sicut Christus quando fuit crucifixus.

'Otherwise,' he added, oblivious of the doctor's expression and a suppressed snort from the boy, 'otherwise one may make three crosses on the wound, and say five *Paternosters*, five *Aves*, and one *Credo*. But I think the first is better.'

'I am affronted,' said Doctor Piper loudly and emphatically. 'First my noble skills are flouted, and with them the skills of my masters – the great Hippocrates, Aesculapius, Aristotle and Galen. Who may you be, young popinjay, to mock such authorities? Shame on you! And then to confound my ears with such vile hocus-pocus, such popish gibberish, as my ears shrink to hear in a Christian chamber. Had you not heard that the

Bishop of Rome no longer rules this land, or that the head of our Church is good King Edward, so young, so wise? I'll warrant both you and this wench are hung about with crucifixes and reliquaries and such mummery, hey?' Under his piercing, searching gaze Alan felt the need to refute the accusation, when it would have been wiser to keep quiet. He pulled out from beneath his collar the modest little silver cross on a thin chain, which had been the gift of his mother in times when the old ways of worship were no sin.

'I wear only this, sir.'

The doctor pounced on Jacquette. 'And you, foolish wench?' Before she could stop him he had dragged out the cross she wore between her breasts, out of sight, suspended from a thong of leather. It was the ivory one which Dame Margaretta had given her; she had kept it as a kind of continuing sign of goodwill between them, and a protection in her adventure. Dr Piper scanned it with an expression of disgust: the exquisite miniature carving of the dying Christ, the radiant Dove over His head that symbolised the Holy Ghost. He made the sound usually rendered as 'Pshaw!' and thrust the cross back into its hiding-place.

'I'll have no more truck with you,' he announced. 'Live or die as you will. Come, Jacob,' and turning on his heel he flounced out, the boy almost treading on the skirt of his long robe.

'And the Devil go with you,' Alan called after him, though not loudly enough to be heard. 'Well, sweetheart, we must find other means. There must be apothecaries in this town still in their right senses.'

Luck guided him to just such a one, in an unlikely alley of old houses, whose jettied upper storeys almost kissed across it. The apothecary seemed almost as old, a tiny creature with a nutcracker face and eyes that were little more than slits, for he was nearly blind. He nodded gently as Alan sought his advice.

'The knife is a terrible thing, my son. You were wise to refuse it for your young dame. I will make you a salve or two that will do wonders for her.' He pottered happily about among jars, seeming to know where each was by touch, compounding this and that with pestle and mortar, humming tunelessly.

'This you must use first, for *heliotropus* stauncheth blood and draweth away poison. Next this, for comfrey healeth. And to soothe both the wound and the sufferer, a salve of cats' valerian. Cats know well to seek out its flowers of rosy purple, for it calmeth their restless spirits and giveth them pleasant visions.'

Taking the three phials, Alan said, 'Sir, my wife is greatly troubled because the wound strikes across her brow. She fears it may disfigure her, and our livelihood depends upon our performances, since we are strolling minstrels and jugglers.'

'Keep the edges of the wound together, and see they are clean. Young flesh heals well, and women have goodly hair to hide a blemish. And for the injury to her leg, use comfrey salve and stint it not.' The fee he asked for his medicines was ridiculously small; Alan put more into the withered little claw, and received a blessing of which Doctor Piper would not have approved. As he left the shop a quavering voice called after him, 'I suppose you would not like to learn how to engender scorpions, or cause serpents to be harmless without removing their fangs?'

'I thank you, not at present, father,' Alan replied. 'Though if our own inventions cease to please we shall gladly come back to you.'

Whether by faith or the virtue of the salves, Jacquette showed a distinct improvement within a few hours. The angry look of the wound began to fade, and the cleanness of the cut made it possible for Alan to press its edges close and keep them so with a linen bandage. He ordered local delicacies to be sent up to her, good broth from one of Dorking's famous hens, a dish of water-souchy, made from various fishes pounded through a sieve and simmered with parsley, and some of the large luscious Dorking snails, delicious when served up with garlic, which were said to have been brought to the district by pilgrims. The invalid's spirits rose with the help of a flask of the local wine, made with wild cherries. She slept heavily and quietly, and Alan was thankful.

Next morning there entered, without knocking, a stout woman, handsomely dressed but coarse of complexion and hands. She announced herself as Mistress Egleton, landlady of the White Hart.

'The servants tell me,' she said without preamble, 'there was a quantity of food sent up yesterday, to wit –' she named every item from a list. 'None of it was paid for.'

Alan agreed. 'It will be added to the reckoning, surely, and paid when we leave.'

'*When* you leave, aye. And how do I know when that be? You're travelling folk, they tell me, that wander the roads like 'Gyptians? And such follow their wills and fancies when it comes to taking leave – sometimes before cockcrow, mayhap?'

Jacquette returned her hard stare. 'If you mean that we would go without paying, dame, you are wrong. We're honest folk of good repute and pay our way. If you want your money now you shall have it – isn't that so, husband?'

'At once, if you like, and when I know how much.'

The landlady thrust the paper at him. From his pouch he produced a little more than the amount. She eyed it askance.

'Not half enough. Besides the food there's the cup of aqua-vitae my good man gave this young woman after the brawl –'

'It was not a brawl!' Jacquette interrupted angrily.

'– and the linen from my own chest of medicines, not to mention the soiling of a sheet with blood so that it can scarce be used again, and more of it on the coverlet, I see, and the pillows, so that this chamber can't be let again unless cleansed and sweetened from floor to ceiling, faugh! Then there'll be a vail to the boy for fetching Doctor Piper.'

'I fetched him myself,' said Alan.

Mistress Egleton appeared not to have heard him. 'And three nights, taking tonight as one, in this neat and private chamber, fit for the King, God bless him, were he to come on progress to Surrey.'

As she paused for breath Alan asked, 'Will this be enough?' and held out a gold royal, a coin still shining new though minted in the reign of King Henry the Seventh, whose image it bore.

The woman's eyes glinted, then were expressionless. She stretched out her hand and pocketed it in her apron. 'Aye, for now.' She left them without a farewell.

'Discourteous bitch!' Jacquette broke out when the door was shut. 'She came to rook us out of our last groat, and so she nearly has. Why, why did you give her the gold? It was far away over what her scurvy board and lodging were worth, and she might have let us off half of *that* in consideration of the fleas.

Ah, *Sacré Dieu*, these thieving English! First Canterbury, now this. *Je m'en . . .*'

Alan dropped on the bed beside her and took her in his arms. 'Love, be quiet, you'll work yourself into a fever. Besides, that woman must not hear you talking in French, or we shall be set down for spies or worse. Let the money go if it pays her off. I was wrong to show it, perhaps – she'd have been content with less. But calm yourself, do.' He rocked her, warm and soft against him, the natural perfume of her hair and skin coming through the after-scent of spilt blood and the herbal fragrances of the old man's salves.

'I should get up,' she murmured. 'I'm well enough to be about, not lying here useless.'

'Not useless.' Alan kissed the white warmth of her neck, beside the ear. 'Most serviceable, and fair and lovely. There's a bolt on the door, I see, and I would not be interrupted . . .'

Languorous in the aftermath of love, she said, 'How well I feel now, and happy. So quickly misfortunes pass over us and we find ourselves in the sun again.'

'So soon.' He smiled, the slow curling smile that had enchanted her at the first sight of him. 'The night may be dark, but the blessed dawn comes at last, to gladden thee and me.'

They had been too rapt in each other to hear stealthy footsteps outside, the footsteps of listeners, who now, suddenly, imperatively, knocked on the door, again and again, till it threatened to splinter. The two on the bed started up in alarm, Jacquette clutching Alan's shoulder.

'Who is it? Who? Don't let them in!'

'I must, since they intend to come in, whether or not.' As he unbolted the door two large men almost fell into the room. Without a word the foremost man seized Alan and held him, while his companion pounced on Jacquette and hauled her off the bed, half-naked as she was.

'A light wench, a giglot!' he exclaimed, delighted, holding her the tighter as she tried to wriggle from his grasp.

'Let that be,' said the first, then called to someone behind him 'Be these they, sir?'

'The very same, the very same,' gleefully answered Doctor Piper. 'I thought the birds had been flown by now, but we're in luck. Take them, and quickly.'

'In the King's name,' said the first man ponderously, 'I arrest you.'

'For what?' cried Alan, struggling. 'For what offence?'

It was the doctor who answered. 'For dangerous subversion – superstition – idolatry – heterodoxy – popery!'

IX
The World begins to end

The stone cell reserved by Dorking for its criminals was small, cold and malodorous. It adjoined the cottage lived in by the jailer and his family, and had at one time been a granary. The only light was supplied by a tiny window, too high up to look out of; the straw on the floor had not been changed for a long time. Alan and Jacquette had been sitting on it, since no other seat was provided, unvisited for some four hours. The striking of a nearby church clock told them the time, every hour seeming longer than the last.

Jacquette, who did not often weep, wept now, tears of anger, frustration and pain. Her head ached and her wound smarted, her injured leg had taken another knock as they had been bundled down the inn stairs and across the street to the cell, which was mercifully only a few yards away. Alan comforted her as best he could, but he too was shocked and furious. All their personal possessions had been left behind, and Alan's plea that someone should fetch the apothecary's salves was ignored by the big fellow who frog-marched him along, to the open-mouthed wonder of passers-by.

'That harridan had knowledge of this,' he said. 'She knew we were to be arrested, so came and dunned us for money first. As for that canting quack, I'd see him hanged and drink a health to the hangman.'

This statement was so unlike the gentle Alan that Jacquette managed a feeble laugh, then began to cry again. 'They burn heretics. Do you think they'll burn us?'

'Nonsense. Stuff. What have we done, to be called heretics? This is all a plot, if you ask me, and that hell-queen Grizel is behind it. *She* has put word about that we use witchcraft, and that prating old whoremaster has seized on it. He's mad, stark mad, but madmen can wreck sane ones.'

They had said all they could say to each other, and were quiet, huddled close for warmth, sunk in dejection. The sounds of traffic and voices filtered into the cell, and mingled noises from the nearby pound, where stray animals were kept, among them a goat, pigs and lost dogs.

It was both a shock and a relief when the key turned and their jailer entered. He was a dry man with few illusions and little time for any classed as criminals, however unjustly.

'Get up,' he said. 'On your feet, and out.' They saw their burly escort waiting at the door.

'Where are we going?' Alan asked.

'Court-house. Appear before magistrate,' and the jailer beckoned his colleague forward. 'Take an arm each, Jack, and don't let 'em loose.'

'We're not like to get loose,' Alan said, 'since my wife is ill and can scarce walk. If you have pity in you, let her go slowly.'

A grunt was the only acknowledgment of his plea, but the man modified his long stride to Jacquette's faltering steps. In pain and humiliation they came at last to the court-house, where, in a large room, darkly panelled, they were told to look sharp and make a reverence to His Worship.

If he had been a two-headed ogre it would hardly have surprised them, on such a day of disaster, but he proved to be a small, thin, gnome-like creature with a nervous tic at one corner of his mouth which, in other circumstances, might have appeared comical. They were too frightened to find it so now. Alan whispered to Jacquette to leave the talking to him, drew a deep breath, and summoned up every ounce of calmness and self-possession he could muster.

Having taken their names, the magistrate enquired, 'M-m-man and w . . .' After several attempts his stutter overcame the word 'wife'.

'Yes, Your Worship.'

'Ha. Hm. Accused of unlawful attendance at m-m-mass. Correct?'

'Not at all, Your Worship, with respect. We attend the new services of the Church, as in law laid down.' Thank heaven, it was true.

This was a surprise to His Worship, who laid down his formidable pen, opened a ledger and shut it again, and then stared very hard over it at the prisoners. 'W-w-w . . . – is that not the charge, constable?' Presented with a sheet of paper covered in Doctor Piper's execrable handwriting, he read, with some difficulty, extracts from it.

'Popish practices. The w-w-w . . . the possession of idolatrous crucifixes. Use of Latin prayers and spells. Conjuration and sorcery. Your answer?'

'With respect, Your Worship, we both wear about our necks small images of Our Saviour on the cross. Surely it's no sin thus to remember Him daily? We worship not the image, but Our Saviour Himself.' Alan was amazed to hear his own voice making these rational statements, which he had not thought out but seemed to clutch from the air. 'As for spells, or incantations, we use no such devilish tricks. The Latin Doctor Piper heard me use was merely an old charm I have known since a child, a prayer that Christ may heal a wound. Can that be wrong?'

'Aye, but Latin?'

'I know no Latin but such rhymes and jingles as that.'

The magistrate pondered. The two before him were unprepossessing enough, the girl scarcely decent (but then she had been hauled from bed, they had said) with a bloody bandage hiding what looks she might have had, and her hair unbound, as was not proper in a married woman. The young man wore odd, over-fancy clothes, unsuitable to his station in life – a velvet jerkin, forsooth, and buttons of silver – and his features had a certain elvishness which might well betoken dealings with the devil. Yet they were both so young, nineteen and almost seventeen, the paper said, and had been brought up for most of their lives in the Old Religion – as who had not, His Worship reflected. He himself found great difficulty in adjusting to the new Book of Common Prayer and the disappearance of the mass. But Doctor Piper was a man much feared in the town, and if these were let off scot-free Doctor Piper would not be pleased, and would make great trouble at the next meeting of the council. He tried another tack.

'You are strolling players, m-m-minstrels. Therefore vagabonds.'

'No, please Your Worship. I have my licence to perform,

here, if you would examine it.' It was a thing from which he was never parted, since without it he could indeed be reckoned a vagabond and subject to whipping and even death; it was his passport to work and freedom. The magistrate barely glanced at it. 'So.' Under his baffled gaze, Jacquette put her hair back and pulled her bodice together over the ivory cross. She looked damaged and young, and not in the least subversive. The magistrate pointed his pen at her. 'How came she by that wound?'

'Please Your Worship, a crazed woman attacked her as she looked to our horses.'

'Ha. Horses. Stolen?'

'Bought, Your Worship, near Faversham in Kent. I have the receipts.'

Since the magistrate could think of no further charge, and had no confidence that there was any case to answer, he cleared his throat, nodded in a knowledgeable way, and said, 'Remanded in custody for later consideration.' Jacquette looked wildly at Alan, who gripped her hand painfully hard and bowed his head meekly. They were not free to go, only to walk by the side of the constable back to the prison.

Back on the cold floor among the noisome straw, Jacquette lay inert, her head on her arm, and slept, worn out. Alan sat up, musing. He had sensed the magistrate's uncertainty, had almost penetrated into that nervous wavering mind. Some sort of fear, not any conviction, ruled the man. His prisoners were guilty, until proved innocent, and his shilly-shallying must not be taken to mean that they were in his *bon-grâce*, cleared of crime. They might languish in that cold cell, listening to bleating, snorting and barking, fed only with bread and water, for a month or more, nobody knowing or caring what became of them, their only company the occasional vagabond or drunkard, flung in beside them to cool off. And Jacquette might die of a festered wound. Alan's thoughts were as black as the grotesquely-large spiders spinning in a corner of the wall above his head.

It was true, what he had told the magistrate: he had little Latin but what he remembered from nurses' sayings in childhood, but they clung fast to the memory, and came swiftly to his help when summoned. He formed words with his lips, not wishing to waken Jacquette.

'*Signum sanctae crucis defendat me a malis praesentibus, praeteritis, et futuris, interioribus et exterioribus.* The sign of the cross defend me from evils present, past, and to come, inward and outward.'

As he murmured the words he wondered, basely, if they would do any good. So many intercessions to so many saints and holy persons, so many candles lit and incense burned, and yet fearful misfortunes continued to fall on the innocent heads of those who so earnestly prayed. Would it not be better if mankind employed itself in trying to right the evils and injustices of this world, instead of concerning itself constantly with the next – which, in any case, promised a great deal of unpleasantness before one came to celestial joys? Why should not the Bishop of Rome, or the Holy Father, just as one preferred to call him, sit down in solemn conclave with the boy king of England and agree together that neither church should persecute the other. Why could they not agree that he who chose to attend mass should do so, that she who preferred the robust hymns of German Luther should sing them to her heart's content without persecution? Our earthly life is so short, reflected Alan; mine may be half over by now, or more than half. Why cannot we poor atomies live together in accord? for the Scriptures say, 'Mercy and Truth are met together: Righteousness and Peace have kissed each other . . .'

At which point in his plan for saving the world Alan realised that he was drifting into an uncomfortable doze, and that he was light-headed. Neither he nor Jacquette had eaten or drunk since supper the night before, and though that had been rich, its memory had faded. He was thinking nonsense, wandering in his mind. Of course it availed to pray, but now he seemed unable to summon up the concentration for it.

A sudden clamour arose from the animal pound; the barking of excited dogs, the squealing of pigs, the frantic mooing of a calf. Alan wondered what had happened to agitate them so much – some knaves of boys stoning them, perhaps . . .

Then he heard it – a low rumbling sound, distant as yet but increasing, infinitely strange and terrifying. He shook Jacquette's shoulder. Startled, she sat up.

'What in God's name . . . what is it?'

He crossed himself. Had his thoughts brought a Judgment?

The sound was louder now, like thunder, yet unlike. There was a crash outside, as a roof-tile slid off and hit the stones of the yard. Jacquette shrieked, and clung to him. There were sounds of confusion in the street, yells and cries, footsteps running, and the din from the pound might have proceeded from several cattle-markets rolled into one. There seemed to be loads of stones falling somewhere, as though from many carts.

'Nous sommes attrapés,' Jacquette gasped. *'Oh Dieu!'*

The key of the door was turned. A woman, pale with terror, confronted them. 'He said there was prisoners,' she panted. 'Make haste, get out. The earth's moving – 'tis the end of the world!' In a flash she was gone, lost among other scurrying figures. From the jailer's cottage came bangs and crashes. Alan seized Jacquette's hand. 'Run! to the inn – over there!'

They struggled through the seething crowd, past weeping women with crying children in arms and horror-crazed men, some on their knees praying. Jacquette forgot her injured leg in the scramble to reach the White Hart, which they found deserted, for everyone was in the street, fearful that the building might fall and crush them. Floors were covered with fallen pots, pans and dishes. At the foot of the stairs leading to their chamber Alan left her and dashed up them, calling back, 'Get the horses! I'll join you.'

She limped round to the stable-yard. Two horses, unharnessed, were running wildly about, but in the stalls she could see Blaise's white nose. Ned was next to him, both geldings rolling their eyes in terror caught from the other horses. Jacquette stroked each and whispered to them soft words of French, *'Doucement, mes petits, mes braves, tout va bien.'* She had just led out Blaise when Alan appeared, carrying the bags he had filled with their possessions. Fortunately each horse was already saddled – it crossed Alan's mind that someone had planned to ride them away and sell them. He helped Jacquette to the saddle, mounted Ned, and said, 'Now. As calmly as you can.'

The horses that had been running loose at this moment, found the way out and took it, joining the crowd in the street to spread confusion and damage with their flying hooves. Alan led Jacquette after them, making soothing noises and patting Ned's neck. Remembering an alley by the side of the inn, he made for it, Jacquette following. Compared with the crowded street it was almost deserted. At a gentle trot they proceeded down it, the crowd-clamour ever fainter behind them. As they reached the end, Jacquette raised her head and listened.

'It has stopped, that dreadful sound.'

'For the moment, yes, but it may begin again. We must get out of the town in case buildings fall. That way – bear left. Open country lies beyond.'

'But if it were to swallow us – if a great crevasse were to split the earth, and we to fall into it! There was such a thing once when my grandfather was in Portugal, a *tremblement de terre*, that destroyed whole towns and buried thousands of people.'

'Better to be buried under good earth than bricks and stones,' said Alan. 'Ride briskly.'

After half a mile or so Jacquette said, 'The horses are not afraid any more. When I found Blaise he was sweating, and now he is calm.'

'Then we need not be afraid, either. But you, sweetheart, how do you fare?'

Jacquette laughed. 'I have not had time to consider. My head and my leg hurt, but I can bear it now that we are out of that place. But Alan, we are so disgraceful, so dirty! When we come to the next village they will stone us. What shall we do?'

Alan pointed. 'That little wood – with good fortune we can find a stream or a pool there, and wash ourselves. I brought everything with me from the inn – our clothes, the salves, our gear for the road – so we can make ourselves decent again.'

Jacquette smiled at him fondly. 'I thought you were a dreamer, husband, but it seems you are a man of action, the strong tree for the little plant to entwine. So I shall be your poor weak little plant.'

'A formidable little plant, my honeypot. Make haste to the wood before we meet anyone.'

Half an hour later, restored to something like their normal appearance, they set out again. Before dusk they found a wayside inn which looked reputable, where they were welcomed, for passing trade was rare. Their appetites, now sharp beyond measure, were satisfied by a supper even better than the one they had enjoyed the previous night. Their bedchamber had an oriel window overlooking an orchard through which meandered a little rivulet. Nightingales sang in the apple trees until dawn, but the two exhausted travellers heard nothing of their music.

Long years after that day, people talked with awe of the great Dorking earthquake. Yet it had only been a small tremor, hurting nobody. Perhaps, thought Alan guiltily, it had been a forceful reminder to him that one should not question the power of prayer, for had he not prayed to be delivered from all ills, especially present ones: and lo, with a great conjuring trick, the prison doors had flown open?

X
Under the Dog Star

Every day of that hot July Jacquette blessed her father for his wisdom in hiding the gold in his black jerkin. It had put them into danger twice, but it had also bought them the horses and good lodgings, and the possession of it meant that Jacquette need not appear publicly until the gash on her forehead had healed. It did this quickly, thanks to her young skin and the apothecary's salves, until from an ugly puckered scar it turned to a pink line. That would never fade completely, but it did not spoil her looks as it would have done across a cheek. The fashionable drawn-back hair-style could do nothing to conceal it, but after much thought, and combing, she devised a style that would: a loop of hair brought forward on each side, forming a frame for the centre of the brow. She hoped it did not make her look wanton.

While Alan performed alone, conjuring, playing the hurdy-gurdy and flageolet and singing, Jacquette rested, glad not to have to face stares and questions, until the idea came to her of buying a piece of black net to drape over her head and face. It gave her a veiled, mysterious look very suitable for fortune-telling with the cards. On an old head it would have appeared witchlike, on a young one it was charming, the more so after Jacquette bought a quantity of sequins and sewed them on the net, where they glittered like stars in a winter sky.

They travelled at leisure out of Surrey, always moving north-west, to be away from the environs of London during this season of the Dog Days, said to be the hottest of the year, caused by the rising of Sirius, the Dog Star. And a lousy old cur he must be this summer, it was muttered, bringing an invasion of long-fanged insects which fretted the leaves into fleshless skeletons, and caused the sun to hide, and heavy grey clouds to shed showers of small frogs upon the earth. It was curious that those one spoke to had never seen this frog-fall with their mortal eyes, but they always knew someone else who had, and could give convincing second-hand detail of how the invaders had made a nuisance of themselves wandering into houses and infesting ponds and wells, and how two women had been frightened into fits by them, not five miles hence.

Even without such awkward and alarming freaks of nature, the Dog Days were unsuited for continual travel on roads, whose every dislodged stone sent up gritty dust. Streams ran sluggishly or were dry, making it hard to find a cool drink or a refreshing wash by the wayside. If some unhappy sheep strayed from the flock and died near the highway, the fact was instantly known to all who passed by, from the intolerable stench. The first greenness had gone from the grass, giving way to a dry brown, and in gardens the first roses were past, and the pretty blues and pinks of summer; now the colours of autumn reigned, yellows and flames, and the birds no longer sang joyously.

Travellers of their own kind were few. The folk of villages and hamlets were not so welcoming as in the spring, and there would be no great festival until the harvest came home. Egyptians and *didekeis* lurked in barns and out-houses, secure in the knowledge that no farmer or landowner dare dislodge them for fear of having his hayrick burnt down or his crops savaged. They contented themselves with stealing livestock, which they would slaughter in quiet spots.

Jacquette lived in apprehension of another meeting with Grizel and her knife, but Alan assured her that one who had made a murderous attack, which might have been fatal, would be far away, at the other end of England, perhaps. 'Does the fox fall asleep in the hen-run?' Jacquette was not so confident. When they met with other strolling people she would ask if the Hooders had been seen, always afraid to hear that they had; though next time she would be prepared.

Alan said they should make for the Thames, where the air would be fresher and gentlefolk from London living in their riverside houses. They were fortunate in finding, near the great castle of Windsor, a harvest-feast in progress at a prosperous farm, with tables laid out in a meadow, and the farmer's family and servants running hither and thither with dishes and flagons. Here they got a good welcome, and a shower of coin for their entertainment. They sang ballads of country joys, of shepherds and haymakers, and played only the merriest of tunes. Then the shepherds themselves came from the fields, washed and spruced up in their best clothes, with flying ribbons. 'Is this St James's Day?' Jacquette asked one of the maidens. 'We lose track of the calendar, on the road.'

'Why, no, mistress, that's four days hence. This is Lammas Day.'

Lammas Day! It was then she should have been married to Gregory Tuke. The thought was strange and daunting, bringing to mind Margaretta Brandon's pride in the wedding-gown, and the unaccustomed tenderness in her voice as she spoke the word 'daughter'. She must be sad, this Lammas Day when so many were merry. Sad, and angry at the ingratitude that had made Jacquette steal away like a thief in the night, leaving only an awkward message that told nothing, gave nothing for comfort to the woman deserted.

That night they slept in a long chamber at the farm, by invitation of the farmer and his wife, with other guests, on palliasses laid on the floor. Those around them were sleeping, healthily tired or cheerfully drunk, but Jacquette lay awake, still haunted by the thought of her heedless flight. Alan touched her cheek, and found it wet.

'Weeping? Why, love – what's to do?'

'Nothing. Pay no heed.' They were whispering, out of consideration for the sleepers.

'Nothing is no answer.'

She told him, falteringly. 'I should not have left my poor dame so, it was cruel. But my mother died when I was so small – I was not to know how a mother would feel if her child . . .' She sobbed against his shoulder, while he murmured consolingly, kissing her hair. But he made no effort to stop her weeping, for such tears did good to the soul, watering it so that it grew and blossomed. The wild wench, who had run away with him against his better judgment, was ripening into a woman. His conscience had troubled him over Margaretta Brandon. One day, when their fortunes were better, they would go back and see her and beg for her forgiveness.

The tears ebbed, but they had made the wound ache, and Jacquette lay awake after Alan slept, listening to the contented snores of the guests round them. Something nagged at her mind that had been pushed out of it by her melancholy broodings.

Suddenly it came, like a stab of lightning. Lammas Day was the first of August. June and July had gone by since the marriage, and she had seen no show, yet had thought nothing of it, *imbécile, tête de linge*! The last few mornings she had been queasy on waking, and today had eaten greedily of the quinces on the table, as though she could never eat enough. There was no doubt that she was with child.

Alan professed a joy he did not feel. To be a father was a fine thing, and a new one to him, but it brought fears with it. Jacquette would not be able to carry on with her part in their performance after a time, and their takings would suffer. Nor was she the rough tramping kind, to travel the roads with a babe strapped in a shawl. The days were gone when *jongleurs* went in groups, always a woman free to look after the children, who thus grew up in a kind of family. And the winter was coming, chill winds and bad roads, when a childing woman should be indoors, warm and sheltered. Heartily Alan cursed himself for allowing this to happen. 'I who can at times foresee the future, willy-nilly, did not foresee what would have been clear to a blind man in a fog. Shame on me.'

But he kissed and made much of Jacquette, who was now all alight with pleasure and excitement. 'Boy or girl, it will have double cleverness, from both of us. A fortunate babe!' Alan agreed, privately determined that the child should somehow have a securer future than the life its parents led.

They earned a little more money than usual in a yard of the Greyhound at Maidenhead, a town whose name provided travellers with inexhaustible amusement. Alan hired a boatman to take them on the river, to Jacquette's delight; she had never been in a boat before, apart from the ship which had brought her and Estienne over from France. She lay back trailing her fingers in the sparkling water, her eyes sparkling as brightly with the secret she shared with Alan, and sang a little song of her own: '*Que c'est beau, Mon p'tit bâteau . . .*'

The heaviness of the weather had lifted, golden sunshine lighting the rich varied greens of the woods clustered thickly on the Buckinghamshire side of the river. They crossed the bridge to the Buckingham shore, travelling at leisure, letting the horses make their own pace, and lay that night at the village of Cookham, under the shade of Cliveden Woods. 'I should like to sleep on one of those islands,' said Jacquette. 'I should like to own one, to build a little house and live there, just you and I and our little *demoiselle* or *monsieur*. We would keep squirrels and dress always in brown velvet and be very, very happy.'

Alan was dreaming. Not of the peaceful scenes they had passed through, but of a cottage whose front door gaped open. Inside it there seemed to be a shape, or bundle, across the threshold. Before it was a stretch of grass on which figures moved jerkily. At first they were not clear, then, horrified, he saw them in detail – men, women and children reeling like drunkards, and weaving in and out among them a skeleton, walking like a living man, carrying in one bony hand a dart or arrow, with which it struck one after another; at which the person struck fell down, lay writhing, and then was still. Then the Thing would stand over the body, grinning; and so on until all lay dead, but for one figure running frantically away.

Jacquette's voice broke in on the horror. 'What ails you? Hush, hush, you'll wake the house.' She was shaking him, striking his cheeks to rouse him. Slowly he crawled into consciousness from the awful vision, his mouth dry with fear. In the dream he had not been able to cry out. He could not, would not, tell Jacquette what it had been, merely that it was like an ugly picture he had seen once, something that had frightened him as a child.

Saddling the horses after they had broken their fast, he said, 'We will stay by the river, not travel cross-country to Reading.'

'But you said there were inns and good houses, and we should not dally about here –'

'I thought again. Second thoughts are best.' Jacquette shrugged. He had been abstracted and unlike himself since waking from the nightmare. But he was the experienced traveller on English roads, and must have his way.

The river led them to Marlow and from Marlow to Bisham.

Then they crossed the border into Oxfordshire, and Alan realised that they were approaching the small town of Henley. He had meant to avoid all towns, but Jacquette had seen the clustered roofs and cried, 'Here are people – now we shall do well.'

There was no choice but to enter the town, for Ned was going lame in one foot, in need of shoeing. The main street was so empty that it might have been Sunday morning and all at church. They soon came to a smithy, but no sound of hammering came from it. Alan, who had been leading Ned, tied him to a post outside, leaving Jacquette to watch him and Blaise, while he called for the smith.

No one answered. He entered the forge, and paused in surprise. The fire was almost out and the place almost cold, like the shoeing-irons. As Alan stared about, a boy rose from a heap of straw in a corner, where he had been crouching. His face was pale and his look unhappy – perhaps his master had recently beaten him. Alan asked him civilly if the smith might be fetched. The boy made no answer, only stared, rubbing his hands together as if he were cold.

'Are you dumb, lad? I asked for your master.'

'In the . . . in the . . .' The boy's teeth were chattering too much for him to speak coherently; instead he pointed through the window to the smithy-house adjoining the forge. Then, with another wild glare, he retreated to the straw and collapsed on it. Alan forgot everything but the lad's evident distress. He went on his knees beside him.

'What's this? Are you troubled? Afraid? Tell me.' He laid a hand on the boy's brow; it was ice-cold. Then beads of sweat began to break out on it, accompanied by a convulsive shudder.

Alan sprang back. 'Holy Jesu!' He ran out of the forge and rejoined Jacquette, who at sight of his face cried out in alarm.

'Ride!' he told her. 'Ride on, out of the town, quickly.'

'But you, what will you . . . Alan, you have seen something terrible, I know it.'

'I'll lead Ned and join you. Go!'

A woman came out of the smithy house and ran towards him, her hair loose and her face blubbered with weeping. 'Master! Master! help us!' she cried. Before Alan could retreat she had reached him and grasped his sleeve. 'My man lies dead in there, and two of our childer. For God's love, fetch a physician – 'tis the sweating sickness!'

'What must we do?' Jacquette asked fearfully. They were in open country again, south of the town, in the sweet air of the river with the Chiltern Hills above them, and no sign of a habitation.

'Do? Why, pray, wife, what else – I for forgiveness, since I was fool enough to enter that town.'

'I persuaded you – I said we could make money there. All my fault.'

'But I had had the warning. I should have known that such dreams never lie. It was the plague I saw, with Death himself striking down his victims. This sickness is not like the other, the Black Pestilence, but it kills more quickly and without many signs. A little pain in the head or arm, then a sweat, and in four hours you are gone. Oh, sweetheart, pray as you never prayed before, for I touched that wretched lad, and the woman touched me and breathed near to me. Fool, fool, fool!'

'Should we not find a church and pray there?'

'No, for that would be enclosed, and sick folk in it.'

'Then we'll pray here, beneath this tree. Three *Aves* and two *Pater Nosters* and a *Credo*, that will do to begin.' It was fortunate that the magistrate of Dorking was not present to hear this sharp divergence from the new Book of Common Prayer. 'And you – have you a charm, like the one you used over me when I was wounded?'

Alan closed his eyes in an effort to remember. Then it came back to him. '"*Ista nomina me protegant ab omni adversite, plaga, et infirmitate corporis et animae* . . ." These names will protect me from all adversities, plagues, and sickness of body and spirit . . .'

But that night, as they lay in the open by the murmuring river, he began to shake and to feel shooting pains in his limbs. He had not, after all, been protected.

XI
The Good Samaritan

'"The hunt is up, the hunt is up,"' sang Sir Nicholas Brome,

'"And it is well-nigh day,
And Harry our King has gone a-hunting
To bring his deer to bay."'

He sang it every time he himself went hunting, in his loud, cheerful, almost tuneless voice. Though he delighted in music he had no ear for it, or much memory for the words, therefore clung to such simple stuff as he had been able to memorise. He also made the same joke every time, a play upon 'deer' and 'dear', with facetious speculation on the late King's six wooings. His servants always produced a dutiful laugh in the right places.

Today he was particularly cheerful, though his chief huntsman had told him there was little chance of taking a hare, and also, as he well knew, that the creatures were out of season. Hunting promoted early rising, lively exercise and an appetite a man might be proud of; he would be out with his beagles at sun-up while strength remained in him, which it well might for a good many years yet. Sir Nicholas was big-framed, stout yet not gross, with a high colour that came as much from fresh country air as from the rich feeding he loved. He had survived infancy without a single ailment – no mean feat in his century – and since then had survived accidents in the field, one shipwreck, and three outbreaks of pestilence.

Added to which blessings, he had had the good fortune to lose his wife, a vinegary lady much given to complaining, after she had given him two healthy sons and a daughter, while he was still young enough to enjoy lustiness and venery. The Brome nose frequently cropped up in villages near Brome Court, the gracious house, rose-red and five-gabled, at the foot of the Chilterns where he had been born and lived all his life.

He owned hundreds of acres of farming and grazing land, two areas of woodland substantial enough to be called forests, and enough rents and tithes to support him amply even without the healthy sum he had been left by his father. A great deal of his wealth went on entertaining neighbours and house-guests from London.

'"With hounds and horn wake up the morn . . ."' Sir Nicholas carolled, breaking off to attend to his man Jem Somers, who, with his mates, followed the beagles on foot. Sir Nicholas, pleasing his own fancy, was mounted. 'Speak up. I can't hear ye,' which was not surprising in view of the cacophony of horn-winding and barking.

'A man, Sir Nicholas. In very bad case. I came on him down by the spring there.'

'A man? What manner of man, and what ails him?' Sir Nicholas reined in his mount. He had an unquenchable interest in all that went on around him. Somers told him that a youth, seemingly ill and distressed, had accosted him and asked his aid, but so incoherently that he had not been able to understand. He had not seemed like any kind of villain or turlupin and was quite safe to approach. Sir Nicholas, nothing loath, set his horse to the trot, and with Somers behind him proceeded to where, in a clump of trees, was an ancient spring known as St Frideswide's Well.

The man who sat by it undoubtedly looked both ill and distressed. His clothes, which were not of country fashion, were covered with grass and hay-stalks. He was hatless, unshaven and dirty-faced. At sight of Sir Nicholas he got to his feet, uncertainly.

'Now, then,' said the knight heartily, 'what's this I hear? Be of good cheer, man, with such a face my beagles might mistake thee for the hare. What's this tale of woe? Let's hear it.'

Alan said, 'Sir. Of your goodness help me. Two days since . . . I think it was two days, but I am not sure . . . as I passed through Henley I took the sweating sickness.'

Somers leapt back, but Sir Nicholas nodded. 'A scurvy thing. I had it myself once.'

'I . . .' Alan paused, summoning the strength to go on. 'It took its course, and thanks be to God I recovered, though weak and faint. But my wife . . . she caught it, and was ill to the point of death. Again we were blessed,' he crossed himself, 'but she miscarried of her child.'

'Tut. A tale of woe indeed. How far was she gone?'

'Two months, we think.'

'So, matters could have been worse. She must be a young thing, your wife?'

'Not seventeen, sir.'

'And where lies she now?'

Alan shook his head. 'I can't tell, sir. My head is so strange and giddy I've lost direction. But some fields away, I think, over there.' He pointed to where the sunrise turned the eastern sky to a great spread of shot silk. 'Near by the river. Our horses are with her.'

'Well, well. Never pull that face at me, Jem Somers. A fellow too craven to aid a poor sick wench is no man for me. I'll tackle the matter myself – run you home and hide under your mother's apron.'

Thus put on his mettle, Jem muttered that he would give a hand if 'twas needed, though he clearly wished he had never drawn his master's attention to the distressed youth. Directing Alan to stay where he was and to make his mind easy, Sir Nicholas cantered off river-wards.

The one he sought for sat under a tree, leaning her back against it like the girl in the woeful ballad. Two tethered horses raised their heads and whinnied at sight of Griffin. Jacquette was hardly recognisable as herself, haggard and starved as she was, tear-stained and frightened. Helplessly she stared up at the big man on the horse. Dismounting, he threw the reins to Jem Somers and approached her, seeing with pity the bloody ruin of her kirtle and petticoat. Here was woman's work, but for the moment it was his.

'Well, pretty one,' he said, with more gallantry than accuracy. 'Your goodman has told me all your case and sent me to fetch you to where you shall have some comfort. Can you walk?' He extended a ham-like hand and helped her to her feet. She looked down at herself with shame, putting her arm before her eyes

'Never heed, never heed,' he said kindly, 'an old wedded man thinks naught of such things. Come lean on me.'

'But the pestilence, sir . . . I had the sickness,' she faltered.

'Marry come up, what do I care for that? I had it too, once, and it can't be suffered twice. Jem, give me a hand here. When I'm in the saddle, hoist Madam up in front of me. Griffin goes gently, my dear, never fear he'll jolt you. So, off we go. Bring up the nags, Jem.' Jacquette, for all her wretched condition, could not forbear a smile at the bluff kindness of this complete stranger. She tried not to think of what her skirts would do to his beautiful riding-boots and buckskin breeches; and it was quite surprisingly easy not to think at all, held in his strong arm and lulled by the movements of the big sure-footed horse. She was almost asleep when she heard him say, 'A swift journey and a good homecoming. Welcome to Brome Court, young Madam.'

With bewildering speed Jacquette was handed over to a large comely woman whom Sir Nicholas named as Dame Dorothy. Exclaiming in horror at her plight, the housekeeper (for such she was) clapped her hands to summon a bevy of women servants. Between them they stripped Jacquette, bathed her and put her to bed in a grand chamber hung with tapestry. Then, from a table laid with damask and good plate, she was fed with dressed beef and wine and spatchcocked pigeons followed by a pie of apricots larded with thick yellow cream from the house's dairy.

While all this was happening, equal care was being taken of Alan by the menservants. Given a voluminous linen shirt of Sir Nicholas's to wear, he was told that clothes would be found to fit him in place of his own, which a servant had gathered up and was bearing away when Alan noticed him, and asked where he was taking them.

'Why, to be burned, as Master ordered.'

'Give me the jerkin back a moment, pray. And lend me a knife.'

'But Master said . . .'

'You shall have it, but first I must take something from it.'

Under the interested eyes of the men, he cut away the stiches of the border and removed the one gold angel that remained of his store. It was to be hoped they were honest fellows, as honest as their master. Soon he was brought clothes of an excellent material and cut, only a little large for him, which he was told belonged to one of Sir Nicholas's sons, Master Simon.

Thus restored to himself but for weakness he was summoned to the presence of Sir Nicholas in an arbour of a pleasant flower-garden.

'Can't abide to be indoors of a fine day,' said the knight. 'Your good wife does well – she sleeps and is watched continually. Your nags have been fed and watered and are stabled with my own. Simon, that's my second son, will see to their exercise, horseflesh being his delight as womanflesh is of other men.'

'I thank you with all my heart, sir. What can I say . . .'

'Pho, pho, say nothing, only sit and tell me how you came here and what is your history, for I love a good tale.'

Alan embarked on an account of his life from its earliest days, Sir Nicholas listening with the keenest attention and enjoyment from beginning to end. Then he said 'And you have both such skills – to dance, sing, conjure, read cards and tell a jest?'

'Indeed, sir.' The knight nodded thoughtfully. Dismissing Alan, he betook himself to the bedchamber where Jacquette slept, watched by an attendant maid. Sir Nicholas surveyed the sleeping girl. Now he saw her for what she was, peaked and thinner than she need be, but as pretty a wench as one might see in a month of Sundays, with the darkness of hair, brows and lashes that he much admired in woman. He had been greatly enamoured of Queen Anne Boleyn, the Night Crow as some called her, as much for her colour as her wit. She, too, had had a touch of the foreign in her voice. He liked the lad's voice, too, and the grace of movement they both had. They brought back his days at Court, gone for ever now. He would be sorry to say good-bye to these two.

But why should he say good-bye? Why should they not remain? He would watch and wait and ponder.

'See she lacks for nothing,' he told the maid, automatically pinching her rosy cheek in passing.

When three days had passed, and the travellers were rested and back to their usual health and spirits, Sir Nicholas bade them stay behind after supper, a meal all the household ate in the Great Hall, which had in its time seen monarchs at their meat. Those of his family who lived at Brome Court remained at table: his elder son, Harry and second son, Simon, and Simon's wife, Agnes. Both sons had much of their father in them; Harry was tall, squarely-built but lean and muscular, with the same Tudor-red hair, a rich russet-gold, and a healthy high colour. A tale ran in the family that King Edward the Fourth, the handsome giant whose beauty had earned him the name of Rose of Rouen, had once slept at Brome Court and left with the then Lady Brome a small souvenir of his visit, which had grown up to become Sir Nicholas's grandfather. The lady, far from ashamed to have born a son of Plantagenet blood, had proudly told him his father's name. The Bromes now kept quiet about their legend – in these days it was not always enviable to have royal connections.

The likeness had missed Simon, who was shorter, plumper and less distinguished in looks than his brother, but had all his father's passion for the life of the countryside, and was reputed to be able to do anything with a horse except make it sing. Agnes, in contrast to the men, was a tiny creature all blushes and giggles, even after a year of marriage. Harry was a widower, but nobody vouchsafed information about his late wife.

Besides these, there was at the supper-table Dame Dorothy, very fine in a silk overgown and a petticoat of embroidered damask, with a large sapphire pendant on the chain about her neck. She would never see thirty-five again, and her ample curves were not disguised by her corset, but it was easy to see that she had been a very pretty girl. She had a merry eye and showed beautiful white teeth in her frequent smile. It was not difficult to guess that she was Sir Nicholas's bedfellow, as well as housekeeper.

Sir Nicholas addressed Alan and Jacquette. 'Tell me, friends, do you like my house? Does it please you? Have you had good care? Do you disfavour any here? Eh? Eh?'

Alan, taken aback, said 'You have been the soul of kindness, sir, and so have been all your people. We shall remember you for ever in our prayers.'

'Nay, do better. Come and live with us at Brome Court. What, are you both owlblasted, and cannot speak?'

Alan, who had been exchanging wild glances with Jacquette,

answered, 'Sir, we cannot afford to live in such state. Even if . . .'

'Who spoke of affording? I mean that you should work for your keep, as my servants and minstrels, getting your clothing, food and firing, and such money as you need to spend. Is that not a fairer thought than tramping the stony roads, at the mercy of every coystril and meacock that chooses to beset you? Beelzebub take me, but have I not as much right as a gentleman in the old time that housed his own players of interludes, rather than take a chance on any jack-clown that came strolling by his gate? You, madam, would you bear your next babe in a ditch, or you, lad, live to be whipped for a vagabond? Reply, reply.'

Even in the short time they had been married Alan and Jacquette had learned the signs and expressions which showed each how the other felt, and were able to talk that language of the eyes which becomes perfect in mature partners. Now they could only discuss the proposition by looks, since Sir Nicholas had not invited them to withdraw and confer. 'Too good to be true,' said Jacquette's eyes to Alan's, and his replied, 'I think him honest, very simple and trusting. There's no guile in him.' To which hers answered, 'It tempts me so much. Would I could believe it.' 'Believe it, then; it can do no harm.'

Being by now perfectly agreed, they took hands, rose to their feet, and saluted Sir Nicholas with a deep, graceful bow.

'We are your humble servants,' said Alan.

XII
Country Matters

At Brome Court time slipped by almost unnoticed, so full were the days and nights. Sir Nicholas was a man with a boundless appetite for pleasure in the form of entertainment. Once he had been able to satisfy it at Court, but in the later years of King Henry's life there had not been the masking and foolery of old times, as the King's ill-health increased and matrimonial troubles oppressed him.

Sir Nicholas, twenty years younger than Henry, hero-worshipped him and modelled himself upon him, unable to see the dark side of the royal character for what it was. It had been shown to him personally once, when he had made a broad jest about their under-the-rose relationship. A dangerous flash had come from those small pig-like eyes, and a growled dismissal had sent Brome scuttling backwards out of the room. Throughout the judicial murders of two fair young Queens, the ruthless chopping-down of Sir Thomas More, and the destruction and chaos of the Dissolution, he had loyally remained blinkered, preserving the image of that golden prince of the Renaissance who had been young King Hal.

When he had reluctantly settled for life in his Oxfordshire home he had at first found it paralysingly dull; one could hunt just so long, then tedium set in, and tedium was a thing he could not bear. So began a determined round of organised jollity, of banquets and parties at which games and charades kept up everybody's spirits until it was time to fall into bed. His hospitality was famous throughout southern Oxfordshire, and with only a little more than thirty-five miles between Brome Court and London it was easy to lure those who could bring him the variety he craved. If a song could be said to sum up his disposition, it was a famous one of King Henry's own composing:

Pastime with good company
I love, and shall until I die,
Grudge who will, let none deny,
So God be pleased, this life will I.

To find himself in possession of two professional entertainers, whose skills would be devoted to all his pleasure, was true bliss. He worked them mercilessly. When no visitors were in the house, then he must have a diversion to make the evening speed by; dancing and songs, or a display of conjuring. He dressed them in liveries of Tudor colours, white and green, and called in Agnes's sewing-woman to devise for Jacquette a costume he particularly admired, a straight flowing robe of light green, embroidered with clove pinks and gillyflowers, with a wreath of artificial blossoms crowning her unbound hair. 'Now I possess a greenwood nymph,' he said proudly.

'He will tire of us,' Jacquette warned Alan. 'When he has seen and heard all we can do, we shall be worn-out toys to be thrown away. Prepare to be flung on the world again.'

'I think him too kindly for that. But we must give him continual change to keep his palate sharp.' Painstakingly they polished every item that seemed to be suitable for the sort of company Sir Nicholas entertained, and raked their memories for anything they might add to the repertoire. Jacquette had learned so many songs in childhood that they had been imprinted on her mind, though she had not sung many of them since her time in London with Estienne, for they were too romantical and delicate for rustic ears. '*Amour si haut*', '*Quand je te veux raconter*', '*Dictes, sans peur*', '*Le joli moys de Mai*' – gentle songs of love and lovers' sighs which had charmed the courts of François I and Henri II. Jacquette sang them more sweetly than ever before, now that her voice was rounded with womanhood. She could silence a noisy company and bring ready tears to the eyes of those already deep in wine.

'Then,' Jacquette said, 'there is "*Le Jeu de Robin et Marion*". In English, *The Play of Robin and Marian*, made by one of our great *trouvères*. It is like your ballads of Robin Hood, but not like – he speaks to her and she to him, and they sing songs, and at last they join hands and dance.'

'I've heard enough of Robin Hood to last me a lifetime,' said Alan, 'and so, I'll warrant, have all who visit here.'

'I might say the same,' Jacquette touched her scar, 'but since we must find new entertainments we ought to perform this, which will be new to the company and is very amusing. My father and mother used to make me laugh with it. And I can remember most of it – I think. Let me see . . . No, I must be quite alone. I shall go to the Knot Garden and rehearse it to myself.'

What her memory could not supply they made up between them, until they had a very lively piece to present for Sir Nicholas's delectation. It was necessary to be lively as well as tenderly amorous, since the gentry (alas) were almost as fond of bawdy as the country folk. For such as enjoyed it, the two minstrels performed such lusty old stuff as 'Watkin's Ale', 'Dainty come thou to me', and 'O Who's at my Window?', besides the songs of country bed-romps, good for a laugh in any company. And it was as well to include songs that everybody could join in, such as '*Caleno custure me*' and 'Walsingham'.

Jacquette mused. 'If we only had a lute . . .'

'Why a lute?'

'It looks so well, so fine, and a deal more fitted to a court than your *chifonie* or the little flute. I shall ask Sir Nicholas for one.'

The knight roared with laughter at such a simple request, and lost no time in riding to Oxford to purchase the best lute to be had there, a Mandora suitable for a lady, its neck sporting a knot of gay ribbons. Jacquette made an enchanting picture (and knew it), seated like an angel in a painting, white fingers plucking the strings, eyes sweetly downcast. As she had foreseen, it improved the whole character of their performances. She thanked Margaretta Brandon in her heart over and over again for having had her taught to play.

Two pairs of eyes were never far from her when she played and sang. Sir Nicholas's clerk and amanuensis was Gideon Baldwin. His background was mysterious, and as he never talked about it, remained so. It was rumoured that he had been brought up for the priesthood, but had left it – even that he was the bastard son of a priest. Dark and pale, he wore his hair cut short, square to his brow, and a neat small beard and moustachio. Some thought his looks Spanish. Very learned, he inflicted his learning on nobody, keeping his skills for his master, who valued him greatly, though he was far from being the sort of Ruffling Boy the knight enjoyed as companion.

When a feast or a revel was toward, none of the household was debarred, down to the last cookmaid, if she chose to wash her face and present herself. Gideon Baldwin loved music. If not absolutely required elsewhere, he would be found wherever it was in the house. However large the company, Jacquette knew that somewhere in it she would see his face, unsmiling, impassive; his gaze fixed on her, and her alone. He did not glance at Alan, who might not have existed for him. It made Jacquette faintly uneasy, but she said nothing. She was paid to entertain, not to have fancies that one of the audience was putting the Evil Eye on her.

The other constant, rapt listener was Harry Brome, whose looks were so handsome that no girl could reasonably complain at catching sight of them now and then. Among slighter men he seemed like a young sun-god, and wherever he was in a company ladies would cluster about him like attendant stars. In the early days at Brome Court Jacquette had found him distant in manner, almost stiff, in contrast with the hearty friendliness of his father and brother, and had thought him haughty and supercilious. Then, finding her one day alone in the gardens, and forced to make polite conversation, he suddenly relaxed his guard and began to talk.

'You grew up in Paris, then, Mistress Thornwood? Tell me of it – I have always longed to see France, ever envying my father for having been at the Field of the Cloth of Gold.'

Jacquette told him: of the Paris of her childhood, Notre Dame with its stone devils, the glorious Sainte Chapelle, the Seine and its *quais* and bridges and islands, and of the late King, *le roi François*, ugly, fascinating, cruel, patron of the Arts and insatiable lover of women, and his beautiful brilliant sister, *la perle des Valois, la Marguerite des Marguerites*; and of the fair child Mary, Queen of Scots, already betrothed to the Dauphin; of the grim Châtelet and its prisoners and loaded gallows.

Suddenly, coming back to the present day, she saw that the

sun was going down behind the hills, making a molten-gold halo of Harry Brome's hair. It had been high in the heavens when they had begun to talk – or rather when *she* had begun to talk.

'Your pardon,' she said, 'I must have wearied your ears with chatter, sir.'

'No, no,' he said earnestly, 'you entranced them. We will talk again,' and with a bow left her wondering that a person should be so suddenly transformed from what she had thought him to be.

After that she had many conversations with him, more than anyone else of the house, for he listened so courteously and with such attention that she found it, for the first time in her life, a positive pleasure to talk; perhaps because he had a better-trained mind than any she had so far encountered. He had been at the University of Oxford, at Magdalen College, and there had been one of a band of young men whose serious amusement it was to write and perform among themselves pieces in imitation of the Latin playwrights Terence and Plautus. These were not sacred Mysteries, such as had been played on carts in inn-yards for three hundred years and more, but dramas and comedies about ordinary humans, kings and commoners, villains and clowns.

Jacquette was astonished and a little shocked. 'But that would be light matter – no more than our *Play of Robin and Marion*!'

'A little more, perhaps,' said Harry with a twitch of the lips. 'They were in Latin, and very high-flown. In Italy students write such pieces to be played in crafted settings, painted to look like rooms or streets, with furnishings and statues and everything seeming real. I would like to see such a performance – and with English speech, though the very thought would have stupefied my learned tutors. I am trying to write one such, but I pray you keep mum about this; my father would think it a womanish sort of pastime.'

Jacquette began to say that nobody who was not blind could possibly consider Harry Brome womanish, but realised in time how immodest that would sound. Wholly masculine were the broad shoulders and slim waist, so well set off by the cut of the stiffened doublet, as the long muscular legs were by the short round-hose, the brown throat seeming browner by the white lawn collar that turned back, like the calyx of a flower, to expose it . . . If people were birds and beasts, Jacquette thought she would be a blackbird, Alan a deer and Harry a lion, golden and majestic. His voice, deep and pleasant, she heard sometimes in her head. She wished he would tell her something of himself – how his wife had died, why he had not married again; for he was the nearest to a friend in a household that treated her, though most amiably, as a singing-girl.

She was happy at Brome Court. Pervaded by kindliness and a wholesome devotion to good living, it seemed an island of peace among the conflicts that troubled England. If she had fancied, when she ran away from Mistress Brandon, that only the wandering life of the road would fulfil her, that fancy was long vanished, now that she had the performer's satisfaction of good audiences combined with a secure, comfortable home, where she was never chidden or bullied, only admired.

One thing in that happy island greatly troubled her. The magic had gone out of her marriage to Alan. Everyone knew that the holy estate of matrimony was not designed as a permanent magical entertainment, but in her thoughtless youth she had imagined that it would be. Yet, though Alan was the same person in substance as when she had first seen him at the fair that May morning, he was no longer the romantic figure who had been her companion of the roads, a young replacement for her dead father.

'The fruit of Love's desire . . .' Alas, where had it gone? Their union had not been blessed with children after the loss of the first. When Alan sought her in their bed it was not with passion, only with affection. Sometimes, herself desirous, she thought that he would have done very well as a monk. If the bawdy songs had any truth in them, there was more to bedding than this.

But to long for it was wicked, when it was her own fault that they had ever wed. They were disparate elements – earth and air, body and spirit. She prayed for forgiveness, and constancy, and to hold him always dear, as she still did. Her punishment must be to know that he was restless, unsatisfied, unhappy.

Alan knew her mind as she did his, and grieved that he could give her not what she craved. Against his will he was growing more and more remote from her. The thing she feared in him, his uncomfortable gift of seeing glimpses of the future, possessed him increasingly. He dared not tell her that some of it seemed to belong to the bedchamber they shared. It was in the oldest part of the house, the remains of a wing built in the earlier part of the last century. Its rooms were small and low-ceiled, with curious carvings of faces and winged shapes on the beams and uprights, which seemed to change form with the changing lights. Jacquette thought them amusing, but Alan avoided looking at them too closely.

He had begun to have a recurrent nightmare. It came at the end of the night, when his deepest sleep was over, and always took the same form. From vague earlier visions he would suddenly think himself awake, and, horribly, not alone in his side of the bed. It was a wide pallet, and Jacquette was lying well away from him, a sad measure of the gulf that had opened between them.

But something was close to him, pressing up against him with urgent nudges, clinging wherever it touched his body, as if with desire. But he knew that it was not desire, or not amorous desire. Then, while he fought it and tried to cry out, it would gradually creep over him until all its heavy cold weight lay on him, stifling, driving the breath out of his lungs, paralysing him with terror so that he could not stir even to make the sign of the cross. A voice, or a thought-voice, spoke repeatedly in his mind, saying, 'Now you are cold but soon you shall be hot, very hot.' They seemed the most fearful words he had ever heard.

He never knew how the nightmare ended, only that he was thankfully awake at last, sweating and shaking with terror, while Jacquette lay beside him peaceful, undisturbed. The loneliness of his fear made him feel even further separated from her.

The servants whom he secretly questioned about the room's history gawped at him. They knew nothing, they said. He hesitated to ask any of the Brome family, in case, expansive as they were, they should mention it to Jacquette, who would then know he had been keeping something from her. It was Gideon Baldwin who told him, knowing the house's history as well as the present-day arrangements of it. He smiled, with lips alone, as he answered Alan's question.

'Indeed it has a tale, the old wing. It was in the days of the Lollard persecution, when King Henry the Fifth reigned, that a woman who had married into the Brome family was arraigned for heresy. Some say the charge of witchcraft was added. She was sentenced to the fire, but her son, who was an earlier Nicholas Brome, pleaded earnestly for her and offered his own life as a surety that she should not spread her poisonous doctrine abroad. The judges relented, allowing him to keep her in house confinement under harsh conditions. Her prison was the room you sleep in – you may still see the marks of bars at the window outside.

'One night, while the rest of the house slept, fire broke out in the old wing and seized on the timbers. When the alarm was given and they went to the place, they were able to save most of the fabric but the woman was dead, burned to ashes. She left a curse on the spot where she died, it's said.'

He smiled again, the dark lightless eyes watching Alan's face.

Alan asked, 'But if the timbers burned, why are the old carvings still whole? I see no trace of fire.'

Baldwin shrugged. 'Repaired, repainted long since. But the curse still holds, I take it?'

'How should I answer that?'

'You have answered it. Your wife has seen nothing, felt nothing?'

'No. And I beg you not to tell her.'

'I shall say nothing. I would not hurt her.'

But you would me, Alan thought. You hate me.

Yet he was unable to keep from telling Baldwin the substance of the nightmare, merely for the relief of telling it to someone.

When Alan told fortunes to amuse the company Gideon Baldwin never came forward to choose a card; only watched, and listened as Alan foretold the most light and likely futures for the Londoners and neighbours who clustered round him. Only when Jacquette read the cards did Baldwin approach.

'Tell my fate, I pray you.' He shuffled and selected cards, from her, as she directed, managing to brush her hand with his. His key-card was the King of Hearts.

Jacquette said, 'You are fortunate. You will get what you wish for.'

'Ah. Good hearing. What will it be?'

She shrugged. 'You know best yourself, sir.'

'A woman?'

'It may be.'

'Or something else?'

Jacquette smiled her most professional smile. 'Others are waiting, sir. I wish you the best of fortunes.'

Neither she nor Alan spoke of this.

The Spring of 1552 brought news from London. Young King Edward was gravely ill, with smallpox and some other disease. Slowly he recovered, but an ugly cough was left, and a wasting which caused people to shake their heads and talk, in whispers, about what it boded for England. His elder sister, Princess Mary, lived retired in her Essex country house, still defiantly celebrating the mass which had been forbidden to her. Her brother knew it, for all the secrecy, and deplored her stubbornness, her clinging to the faith of her dead Spanish mother. 'Mulish Mary', some laughingly called her: one day she would bear another more terrible nickname. Surely, they said, the strongly Protestant Edward would never leave his throne to her.

Nor did he. In the year that followed he knew himself to be dying, and bequeathed throne, crown and kingdom to Lady Jane Grey, third in succession after Mary and the young Elizabeth. Poor little Jane, that learnèd child, was a pawn in the hands of her unscrupulous father-in-law the Duke of Northumberland; she had no choice but to take the most unwanted gift.

When Edward at last faded into death, only fifteen, the excitement at Court was such that Sir Nicholas itched to travel to London to be in the midst of it.

'That little wench will never reign, mark me. Crown her, you crown her fox of a father-in-law too. I wouldn't give a false groat for her chance, no more than a cat in hell's.'

'Why, who's to stop her?' enquired Simon.

'How the devil do I know? Northumberland himself would cut his own mother's throat in a church if it would advantage him – why not his daughter-in-law's? And Her Sowship of Suffolk hates daughter Jane, it's said. Or there's Young Bess at

Hatfield with her nose out of joint; she's not without friends. But my guess is Mary, a lemon-faced vixen only a blind man would bed, though she was well enough as a wench. What's there left for her but to be Queen, even if it takes a rebellion to do it?'

'She might rather wish to be a nun,' Harry said, 'pious as she is.'

'A nun, with a crown dangling before her? Let her come in sniffing distance of it, and 'twill be a fico for nunneries. How her good old father ever came to sire such a brach is beyond me; but there, Spanish blood on the mother's side, no trusting it.'

Harry, who did not share his father's admiration for the late King Henry, observed that Princess Mary's father had been just as self-willed, and more so, not caring who was mown down so long as he got his way. 'Thus he severed us from the Pope and killed those who dissented.'

'Aye, aye, true enough. Let Lady Jane look to her neck.'

Agnes looked sharply up from her sewing. 'But, sir, she is no more than fifteen, the same age as was King Edward, God rest his soul. Who would kill such a child?'

'Wait and see, daughter. Wait and see. Blood will flow on Tower Hill, and some of it will be that lass's.'

Agnes shivered. 'Don't talk of such things – I felt the babe jump with fright. Would you have it miscarry, or be born with a bloodmark on the cheek?'

Harry threw an affectionate, protective look towards his small sister-in-law, all the tinier-seeming now for being eight months gone with her first child. 'Leave it, father. We shall know soon enough, and it may fall out better than you think.'

But the next news brought to Oxfordshire was that Princess Mary had shut herself up in her Suffolk castle, ready to defend it against all comers, and that Northumberland had marshalled men and ships to crush her supporters.

'What did I tell you?' said Sir Nicholas triumphantly. 'Such a fray is coming as you young ones never yet saw.'

XIII
New Crowns for Old

Agnes gave birth to twins on a sultry day in August, three weeks before they were expected. The boy and girl were, as the midwife said, scarcely bigger than mice, but that was only to be expected, and it was a blessed mercy that all three, mother and babes, had survived, for now Master Simon had two for the cost of one, and the dam brisk and willing to fill next year's cradle.

But on the fourth day the tiny girl sickened, and the rejoicings, which had been going on since the birth, were halted. The tenants and neighbours from surrounding hamlets who had been filling themselves up with Sir Nicholas's ale, bread and groaning-cakes and pasties went soberly home, while the family gathered round the baby, and Agnes wept.

'Alas, she's going,' said Dorothy, who had been the midwife's assistant. 'Look how the lips turn blue, poor scrap.'

Agnes cried from her bed, 'Is she baptised? Has any of you called in the priest?'

Nobody had. Sir Nicholas detested the local incumbent, a man of few words who resented the change-over to Protestantism he had been forced to make, and gabbled through the new Book of Common Prayer with hurried distaste. The Brome family and servants dutifully attended his church, but he was popular with nobody but Gideon Baldwin, who visited him often. Sir Nicholas read morning and evening prayers in the little private chapel of the house – hurriedly, as the priest did. He was not a pious man, no more than the next, but these usages must be kept up even when they were new-fangled. As to the rite of baptism, it was essential above all things, for if the babe died before it, the soul would go to Limbo, that dismal region on the border of hell, in which no mother could bear to think of her child.

Dame Dorothy bent over the cradle, distraught to the depths

of her motherly heart. 'I did all I could! I gave her a sip of cinder-water for her first drink, and carried her upstairs before down. Why should she be taken?'

'Never question,' said Simon. 'Bring her to the chapel and she shall be christened without the priest.' Hastily the dying child, faintly mewing like a kitten, was wrapped and gathered to the nurse's bosom to be carried downstairs. Agnes wept so bitterly that Jacquette stayed to comfort her; she more than any there knew what it was to lose a child, even one unborn.

The chapel was crowded with weeping servants. There had not been a death in the house since that of Sir Nicholas's lady, almost twenty years before. Apart from the young father, Sir Nicholas himself was most affected. He had two grandchildren already from his married daughter Meg, but the twins were the first babes to be born in his house for so long, and he had been so exultant that both had survived. He fumbled with the prayer book, failed to find the place, for his eyes were tear-filled, then thrust the book at Harry.

'One of you read it. I can't.'

Gideon Baldwin stepped forward. 'I can recite it quickly.' He began to rattle off Latin in a clerical monotone, but Harry intervened.

'We'll keep it lawful, if you please. Master Thornwood, you read well and clearly. Take it.'

'I am no priest –' Alan began.

'I asked for a reader, not a priest. You will stumble less than I.'

Unwillingly Alan took the book, and recited aloud in his clear, trained voice the service he had never before read.

' "Dearly beloved, forasmuch as all men are conceived and born in sin . . ." '

He read quickly, for Dorothy was looking down pitifully at the child, who was quite silent now. Seeing a long passage coming, he skipped to the most important part of the service, in which the godparents were invited to promise certain things on the child's behalf, and to name it. Dorothy and Sir Nicholas presented themselves as godparents, and said that the babe's names were to be Elizabeth Dorothy; Elizabeth for her dead grandmother. Then, with the water hastily fetched in a bowl,

Alan signed the tiny brow, saying, ' "I baptise thee in the Name of the Father, and of the Son, and of the Holy Ghost. Amen." '

There seemed no sense in reading any more, for the godmother's face told him all. The women laid the little body down on a bench, unwound the shawl that wrapped it, and put on it the white linen chrism-cloth which denoted that it was now a Christian, and which would be its shroud.

Sir Nicholas led a prayer, and the company filed sadly out of the chapel. Alan and Gideon almost collided in the doorway. Gideon waved him forward with a mocking bow, saying, 'After you, Sir Parson.'

'I am no parson,' Alan retorted. 'I had no wish to read. You could have said the service, for me.'

'Ah, but that would not have done, would it? Since we must hold to the New Religion. You must not forget to ask for the shilling – the parson's fee. It would mean much to the like of you.'

'Why do you so hate me?' Alan asked, though he knew. The other smiled sardonically, without replying.

The surviving twin, Nicholas, known as Nick, was almost a year old, a thriving jolly infant who had soon outgrown his early delicacy, when a horseman rode up to Brome Court just as Harry and Simon were returning from a gallop. Harry recognised with pleasure a friend of his Oxford days.

'John Berkeley! Welcome, welcome. What good errand brings you here?'

'News, Harry, news.' Dusty and stiff with riding as he was, Berkeley could not keep it to himself for longer than it took him to dismount.

'It's all over. Princess Mary is proclaimed Queen, and lodging in the Tower to await her coronation.'

Harry whistled. 'And Northumberland, and Lady Jane?'

'In the Tower too – as prisoners. He's charged with high treason, and she . . . it remains to be seen what mercy she gets.'

Within the house, rested and refreshed, John Berkeley told them all more. 'Northumberland's army got never a cheer as they marched to Suffolk, and his fleet deserted to Mary. He lost his courage and pitched camp at Cambridge, waiting for Mary's troops to disband and go home. Instead of that they marched on London, and into the City, where the people cheered like mad for her and rang all the bells. No question of it, she'll be crowned within weeks.'

Sir Nicholas said, 'Princess Elizabeth?'

Berkeley made a prim face. 'As ever – mim as a mouse all the time the risings and contentions were on, then came meekly out to kneel to her sister. But there's no love lost there; she'll need all her cunning to keep her head.' Berkeley leaned earnestly over the table. 'I tell you, Sir Nicholas, I don't like it. Mary's popular now, because the people knew her when they knew nothing of Jane, and with her the crown stays Tudor – but how long will the kissing last? I saw her close when she came into the Tower, as close as I see you, and hers is not the face of an ordinary woman.' He looked from one to another of the feminine faces around – Agnes, dollishly, quaintly pretty, Dorothy, rosy-cheeked and plump, and Jacquette, darkly lovely, a face he could have looked at long.

'She seems older than her thirty-seven years,' he said, 'her skin yellow, lined and dried up, her lips shrunk to a straight line. Her eyes peer sharply, being short of sight, and have a hard look like pebbles.'

'You judge severely, John,' Harry said. 'A lady of middle years and more is not likely to be a tender beauty.'

'It was not beauty I looked for – it was gentleness. They say she cares for nothing but her religion, and will lose no time in bringing the country back under the power of Rome.'

'What's the matter with that?' Sir Nicholas asked. 'We were pleasant enough in the King's time, before he kicked the Pope up the . . . kicked the Pope. It would be mighty comfortable to have an old-fashioned priest again, instead of that jackanapes of a parson.'

'You spoke harshly of Mary, sir,' Agnes reminded him. 'You said she was lemon-faced and a vixen.'

Sir Nicholas looked uncomfortable. 'I may have spoke too sharp, daughter. What's a fair outside, when all's said? The heart, the heart is all.' But what he had said before was only the truth; he had never cared for his idol's elder daughter, a little stunted thing with none of her father's grandeur and early charm, always telling her beads and surrounding herself with long-faced Spanish priests. She'd have done a good deal better to have altered her ways and shown some charming submissiveness, in Sir Nicholas's opinion. He had always preferred her half-sister, the enchanting Boleyn's daughter. Elizabeth had none of her mother's fatal lure but bore herself like a very Tudor and had a fair white skin and exquisite hands made for jewels and kisses, even if she were awesomely clever, beyond what was fitting for a young woman.

On the whole he was not too troubled by the changes that would certainly come. He and his household had conformed before, they would conform again. He suspected that the English people in general were much like himself, not particular what they said in church so long as life went along merrily enough outside it. He was sure the joys of heaven would not come up to a fine day out with the beagles.

Very few changes did come in the first months of Queen Mary's reign. In February of the next year she was persuaded, against her first decision, to order the execution of Jane Grey and her boy husband, as a matter of expediency, though the condemned Northumberland pleaded for them, innocent and young as they were.

Two months later the Government introduced a Bill under which the Queen would have the power to order the burning of any person who had been condemned as a heretic by an ecclesiastical court or royal commission. And in July she married Philip, Prince of Spain, a widower eleven years her junior. From that day of very mixed rejoicing, the signs came ever thicker and faster that Queen Mary, now backed by the power of Spain, was determined to reunite her kingdom with Rome. By Christmas the field was clear for her to burn as many heretics as she liked for the good of their souls and the general welfare of the realm.

In the Christmas festivities at Brome Court the old services were used, conducted, to Sir Nicholas's disgust, by Parson Jackson, the jackanapes, almost jovial now that he could call himself a priest again. Gideon Baldwin acted as his server and altar-boy. After Twelfth Night Gideon asked Sir Nicholas's leave to absent himself from his duties for a short time, perhaps a month.

'If it will not incommode you too much, sir. I would like to make a . . . I might call it a sort of pilgrimage.'

'Ho! Bare feet and a turned-up hat wi' a scallop-shell? No use trudging to Walsingham and Canterbury, you'll not find one bone to worship.'

Gideon smiled. 'Not so, sir; just a matter of personal business, and to revisit some old acquaintances.'

'Well. It *is* damned discommoding. Could you not have undertaken it over Christmas? I tell you what, I shall let the figure-work pile up to vex you when you come back, and in the meanwhile Alan Thornwood shall write my letters, since he of all the house writes a fair hand.'

The absence of Gideon from Brome Court was a welcome relief to Jacquette. The place felt lighter, the air clearer; she sang about the house knowing that no dark-bearded face would confront her round the next corner. It was not that he menaced her, or ventured any familiarities, but she was always conscious of the probe of those cold dark eyes and the unnatural attention he paid to every moment of every performance. There were times when she wanted to laugh wildly or commit some folly that would at least shock him.

In the freedom of his absence she told Alan of her feelings, hoping he might offer to exercise his right to protect her from annoyance. But he said, 'What can I do? If he never touches you, never insults you, there's no case. You are there to be stared at, after all, and he has as much right as anyone.'

'Oh, you applaud him, then? I see it now – we're so long married that you care nothing who stares at me, or how,' Jacquette said bitterly. 'I was a new trick for you to learn, and now am learnt by rote and of no more interest, so other men may do as they please with me – toy with me, bed me, I suppose?' He said nothing, so near the truth were her harsh words. Afraid of a painful quarrel, she tried to mend things. 'You're weary. This clerking has tired you out. Think no more of my *bavardage*.'

'I thought all your French was forgotten,' said Alan with a mirthless smile, and began to talk of something else.

The clerking indeed wearied him, but no more than the life he led every day. He longed to escape to freedom, away from the safe dullness, the amiable dull people, away from Jacquette. Their first meeting had been magical, and what had sprung up between them utter enchantment. Now there was familiarity and fondness, and the satisfaction of working with a true professional, but no more, alas. To her the life of the country house, the admiration of the guests, the friendship of the family, were all; to him they were nothing.

I am a thing captured and enslaved, he thought, a beast that should have freedom to go where it will and live by what it can get. Jacquette is as she sees herself, a blackbird, a plump pretty ousel, singing songs for its food in a garden enclosed. And yet we must be mated, living as creatures of the same kind, against nature's laws.

It was in these dark days of winter that the thought came to him. In the spring he would go. He had made no promise to stay at Brome Court for ever; Sir Nicholas would have no choice but to release him. Jacquette might weep and scold, but she would be better without him, her bright spirit no longer tarnished by his. He would go back to the roads, with better skills than he had had before, travel to new places and polish his wits among new people. He would see again the golden villages of the Cotswolds, the countryside north of London, perform in houses that were not the one which had become a tedious prison, and held a room where some chimera or devilish succubus made his nights terrible.

He began to make plans.

Jacquette felt the distance between them growing. She tried to talk, to question him, but met always with silence and evasion. After an argument that turned into a quarrel, she ran in distress to the parlour that was Dorothy's own, a pleasant room overlooking the Knot Garden, with an oriel window built out to form a seat where Dorothy and Agnes would sit sewing and gossiping; they formed a harmonious army of two against the forces of their menfolk.

She found them there, Agnes curled up like a little girl with her feet tucked under her skirts, Dorothy's ample form taking up the rest of the space. Both had needlework in their hands, but were more intent on young Nick, who was busily crawling round the floor investigating everything of interest within his reach.

'Lord save us!' cried Dorothy as Jacquette entered. 'What ails thee, poppet? Come then.' She held out her arms. Jacquette ran to her, the floodgates of her tears opened by sympathy. The women made room for her on the window-seat, where, with Dorothy's arm about and Agnes's hands holding hers, she sobbed out her woes.

'Alan loves me no more. He speaks harsh. I can't please him, whatever I do. Just now he looked at me as though I was an enemy. Oh, what shall I do, Dame, what shall I do?'

Dorothy soothed and patted. 'Men are kittle cattle, child. It was some whimsy that took him and he spent it on you, as they will. Many a time have I borne the brunt of it when somebody has crossed Sir Nicholas, and so will Agnes tell you of Simon. Yet we must bear all cheerfully, for a smiling face does as much as the blessed sunshine for a black humour.'

'But it was not just a passing humour, Dame. It has been with him now for weeks – months, perhaps.'

'He may have some illness, and scruples to tell you,' Agnes suggested.

'That might be so . . . yet he seems well enough, and I should surely know, being with him night and day. No, it is not that.'

Dorothy said carefully, 'Might it be that another face has taken his fancy?' The thought had never struck Jacquette; even now it seemed barely possible.

'It could be so. Yet he has never looked twice at any of Sir Nicholas's guests. Or seemed to. Has some double-dealing gone on behind my back, I wonder?'

Dorothy had a wide experience of errant fancies on the part of Sir Nicholas; double-dealing, exchanged glances, unexplained absences, and infants seen about whose family likenesses were unmistakable. She had learned, after some pain and tears at the beginning, to bear it all with outwardly unflinching good humour, and not a cross word spoken. It had also taught her to detect the symptoms of a wandering fancy and a lustful itch in any male creature. It had enabled her to nip in the bud several troublesome situations in the kitchen and dairy. It had assured her that Simon was faithful to his Agnes. Now she wondered if it had misled her about Alan and Jacquette. On the whole she thought not.

'The ladies hereabouts are known for virtue,' she said, 'and if some who come here from the Court have a rolling eye and an overmoist palm, they take them hence quickly enough. Your man can scarcely be pining for Agnes, and most assuredly not for me!'

Agnes giggled. 'What I carry in here is Simon's, and so will all the rest be.' She patted her swelling kirtle. 'Could that be what ails Alan – that you have no babe?'

Jacquette watched Nick in his progress across the floor. He was now getting dangerously near the fire, but he had stopped to chew a twig of kindling, which was good for his emerging teeth. She shook her head. 'I would know that. And when I miscarried it was for me he was troubled, not for the babe.'

'I thought it might be with him as it is with Harry.'

Dorothy shook her head in warning, but Agnes prattled on. 'His wife Joan was very young when they were wed, younger than me, and so beautiful you never saw any to touch her. A bonny couple they were indeed. Well, she was with child almost as soon as the stocking was thrown and the bridefavours given out. But when her time came her travail was fearful – for three days and three nights it went on, though every single knot in the place was loosened and a piece of old bell-rope tied round her middle, as the custom is, but still the child would not be born, and her crying would have melted a stone, poor lamb. (I was betrothed to Simon and was her bosom-friend, so they let me be with her.) Harry never left her side all the time, though of course men should not be permitted in the birth-chamber. And when she died at last –'

'Agnes, you talk too much,' Dorothy said. 'These things are not to be spoken of in this house, and well you know it. Jacquette, what this babbling girl would say is that Harry grieved more bitterly than was natural over Joan and the dead babe – called himself a murderer and what not, until we thought him fit for the madhouse. Afterwards, when he came back to his wits, he made a vow that he'd never again risk a woman's life in bearing his child. So he'll not marry again, and Sir Nicholas is still in the mumps about it, and Nick here is to be his heir.'

'*I* should not mind at all if Nick were not to inherit,' Agnes said. 'He'll have plenty, and so shall we all, and I'd as lief Harry's son had Brome Court, then Simon and I could live at Henley, which is a merry-go-round to this place.'

Nick crawled to Jacquette's feet and began methodically to prise a silk rosette off her shoe. She watched him, her thoughts busy. So this was the reason why the gorgeous Harry Brome had not married again, and why he was so stiff and formal with women. The tale had the good effect of taking her mind off her own troubles for the moment.

On that very day, in a village a mile or two from Oxford, Gideon Baldwin sat in an alehouse. His rustic companions were noisy, even riotous, since he had just bought drinks all round, and in any case it was a holiday, Plough Monday. Outside in the yard stood a beribboned and part-gilded plough, dressed with evergreen boughs, the Fool Plough, which would be dragged from house to house by a shouting company, also hung about with ribbons and led by the Bessy, a man dressed in woman's clothes and a cloak of skins; his function was to collect money. By the end of the procession all concerned would be laughing-drunk. Gideon's business with them was best undertaken while they were still sober enough to understand questions, and answer them.

'Now, good friends,' he said, 'a word, if you please.'

XIV
The Hunt is up

They clustered round him, this dark-garbed stranger who was so free with his money, a ring of rustic faces: brutish, simple, coarsened to the texture of leather with wind and sun, gap-toothed and grinning with pleasure at this extra treat on a festive day. There were a few women, transformed by work and weather almost out of the semblance of womanhood, and a yellow-haired youth like a chicken, bold enough to have pushed himself in among his elders.

'I ask you only a little favour,' said Gideon. 'Can any of you tell if mummers from other parts are like to join in your frolic today? Dancers, jugglers, any of that sort?'

In the long silence his audience cudgelled their brains almost audibly. Then one said, 'There be the Morrisers. But us knows them.'

'Fiddler came year before last,' another offered.

'Aye. But not last, for 'twere neck-deep in snow. Oi did get moi cart stuck, best part of three week.'

When it was clear that nothing else would be forthcoming, Gideon gave up and resigned himself to lingering for long enough to see whether any strangers arrived. Outside the ale-house the air was still and biting, frost lying hard in the rutted ground. Pigs and fowls, usually eager to wander about among any gathering in the hope of scraps, lurked in shelter, the patient oxen rested in their stalls while their torment, the plough, made holiday. Gideon was glad of his fur-lined cloak, though it was only rabbit-fur, and of his stout thigh-boots. Sir Nicholas's pay was generous, for the times.

From its starting-point outside the church, the procession wended its way towards the next hamlet. A score of men yoked themselves to the Fool Plough: not only the local ploughmen, but others from outlying farms, all wearing their best and decked out with what finery their wives had found to pin on them – a bunch of corn in the hat, saved from harvest for this very day, a scrap of bright cloth, an animal's paw roughly gilded, and ribbons of every colour.

Behind, in a straggling train, came others carrying the tools of their trade – threshers with flails, reapers with sickles, carters bearing long whips which they frequently cracked to add to the merry noise, while the smith walked proudly in his singed leather apron and the miller in garments symbolically spattered with flour. As they marched they sang, or bawled, the song 'Speed the Plough', while some blew cow-horns and the Bessy rattled his money-box and pranced so high that his short skirts flew over his head, to the uproarious pleasure of those who walked beside the procession. He also made much play with the bullock's tail attached to the back of his gown.

Gideon strolled along with them, unsmiling, uncaring for the stares he got. They took him for some Oxford scholar out for a day's merriment, though he showed little sign of feeling any. At a prosperous farm, some four miles from the village, his long walk was rewarded. The procession came to a halt outside the door, where the farmer, with his wife, family and servants were waiting; the drawers unyoked themselves, their followers laid down their implements, and cheers arose as maids came among them bearing bread and cheese and mulled ale. The Morrisers shook their bells and capered, then came a call for a Hey-go-down, and suddenly everyone was dancing, flinging, cavorting, hand in hand, arms across, up the middle and down again, with shouts and laughter.

Amid the noise Gideon did not at first notice that they were dancing to music. Then, sweet and sharp, through the din came the sound of a fiddle. The fiddler himself stood on a pile of frozen sacks that still only brought him up to the height of the shortest person there. He was a tiny man, child-size, nutcracker-faced and twinkling-eyed, the very spit and image of an elf, who might have played for the revels of Queen Titania, while Robin Goodfellow acted as Master of Ceremonies. As his bow swept across the strings he smiled a wide cat-smile, his little head in its leather cap moving to the music of the jig. Gideon watched him intently.

When the dance finished and more ale was going round, he moved to the fiddler's side and tapped him on the shoulder. 'Good day, friend.'

'And a merry day to you, master.'

'You make fine music.' Gideon slipped a coin into the pouch which hung, ostentatiously open, at the fiddler's belt.

'Thankee kindly, master, 'Tis my pleasure as well as my trade.'

'You speak like one not of these parts.'

'Of Wales, master. In Clyro was I born, under the hill and by the castle of the old Romans. You know it, hap?'

'Not I. You travel far, following this trade of yours?'

'Far as I can. For is man a plant, to put down roots in one earth? I go where my music takes me, to fair and Whitsun-ale or whatever, and where I go I get a welcome, which not every man can say.'

'You meet many more like yourself – musicians, players, folk who live by entertaining? I would meet with a certain band who go about as you do, playing *The Mask of Robin Hood*, and call themselves the Hooders. Do you know them?'

The fiddler's eyes flickered. 'I might, and again I might not.'

Gideon produced another coin. 'What would be the price of your knowledge?'

'Thirty pieces of silver?' The little face was sly. 'We travelling people don't care to betray each other.'

'I mean them no harm, I promise. I would only speak with them, to learn something – something that would aid me to get a thing that is rightly mine.'

'Many play *The Mask of Robin Hood*. I might tell you of one band, and it would not be the one you seek.' His piping voice was in danger of being drowned by the voices calling on him to play another tune. 'Let our fiddler go, master!' cried a girl, plucking at Gideon's sleeve. 'Us wants to dance, 'tis too cold for chatter.' Gideon saw his chance of information slipping away, and pressed the coin into the pedlar's hand.

'Try to remember. There's more reward if you can.'

'Well . . . now. Would there be a Friar with a belly that needs no stuffing outside, being well stuffed within, and a tall Robin with a good green jerkin?'

'I know nothing of the men,' Gideon said impatiently. 'The girl, the Marian, what is she like?'

'Ah . . . This one, as *might* be what you ask, she's a long-leggity mort, black hair hanging down to her bum, a face not fair but having the . . .' he screwed his face into something between a leer and a broad wink, lewdness itself. 'And a shrew, they say, not that I ever felt her nails.'

'A half-gypsy?'

The pedlar shrugged. 'Born in a ditch, hap, but no true Romany.'

'And her name is Grizel?'

'Aye.' He had said enough, or too much; he began to tune his fiddle. Gideon caught his arm. 'Where can I find them, and when? Quickly, tell me!'

'How should I know, master? But – you might try Thame, or Reading, at Shrovetide. And the devil's luck go with you,' he added under his breath, misliking the aspect of his questioner. As he raised his fiddle, the bow poised, curiosity moved him to ask, 'What is it, master, this thing that is rightly thine?'

Gideon answered, 'A jewel.'

It was the jewel herself, the girl he craved with a consuming hunger, who had reluctantly told him how she had come by the scar on her brow. Subtly he had probed for details, and got them, until she grew suspicious and cut him short.

Now he would follow where the fiddler's hints led him.

The Shrovetide of 1555 saw the last careless merriment England would know for years to come. Mary the Queen was pregnant, or so she gave out, a miracle considering her age. In the previous November she had felt the child leap, the child which would effectively exclude her troublesome sister Elizabeth from the succession and ensure that the Catholic religion would be preserved in England even after its mother's death. It had been intelligent and precocious enough to make its premature move (for it was only two months in the womb) when Cardinal Pole arrived from Rome as Papal Legate, and Mary set eyes on the cross he carried.

But some whispered, behind closed doors, that the Queen was mistaken. The French ambassador had heard from a friend, who had heard from another friend, who had heard it from the Chief Royal Midwife, that the Queen had no other symptoms of pregnancy beyond a swollen figure, and that in her (the midwife's) opinion the doctors either knew nothing about their trade or knew the truth and were lying in their teeth because they were afraid of the royal fury.

For maternity had not softened the Queen's attitudes. She could be merciful to her enemies – she had debated quite a time before deciding to have Jane Grey executed, and some monarchs would have had Elizabeth's head off long before now. But heretics were a different kettle of fish. They were committing treason against God Himself, inciting others to do so, and putting their immortal souls in peril. It was her bounden duty to exterminate them by the cleansing fires that would reduce their sinful bodies to ashes and send their rescued souls happily off to Purgatory for a thorough purifying before they could be admitted to a Catholic heaven.

The fires were lit in February, with the burning of John Rogers, a Protestant leader who had helped to translate the Bible into English. He was a married priest, a shocking thing to be in Mary's eyes, so his request to see his wife and children before he died was very properly refused.

After Rogers went John Hooper, Bishop of Worcester and Gloucester. They took him home to Gloucester, to suffer in his own diocese, and the Queen ruled that he was not to be allowed to address the people, as was usual, in case he slipped in some Protestant propaganda. The fire burned poorly; it took the Bishop three-quarters of an hour to die.

Another bishop followed him to the flames – Ferrar, Bishop of St David's in Wales, who had been a favourite with young King Edward.

The tales that got back to Brome Court were so terrible that the younger folk could scarcely believe them. Such horrors had been heard of, but not in their lifetime.

'But it hurts so, even to burn one's finger!' Jacquette cried. 'How must it feel . . . I am sick when I think of it. Are not the pains of hell burning, that they preach of? If that is true, how is the devil worse than man?'

Alan said little, but there was turmoil in his mind, and the black melancholy which had been stealing upon him settled round him like a cloak. In dreams he saw constantly the flicker of flames against swirling smoke, and felt a menace that transcended any fear he had ever known.

And the words of the nightmare voice sounded in his head.

Sir Nicholas refused to be infected with the general alarm.

'Be of good cheer, my children, for who can point the finger at us? We celebrate mass again, we have gone back to the old usages in public, whatever we please to do in private, and I for one shall tell my beads or not, as the humour takes me. Besides, who'll trouble to seek us out, in this retreat?' He caressed the great head of a hound, who slobbered and gazed sentimentally up at him. 'Let 'em poke and pry in London.'

'They'll poke and pry where the Queen thinks fit, Father,' Harry said. 'It would be wise to call the servants together, farm-hands and all, and warn them to behave as if there were watchers everywhere.'

'But why? What bishops and clerics have we in this house?'

'None – I thank God. But the Queen's net is taking in smaller fry now – humble folk that speak out of turn. I'd not meant to tell you, but when I was in Oxford last week I heard of a carter who spoke against the Pope in liquor. They carried him to the Bocardo prison and questioned him while he was still too drunk to know what he was saying. The day after that he was burned. You may well look pale. Once zeal has taken hold it rages like a fire –' He checked himself. 'Not a happy phrase. But so it does.'

Agnes sighed. 'Perhaps if there had been a child it would have softened her, but months have gone by, and it has come to nothing, poor thing.'

'Poor thing?' Harry turned on her. 'That would have set the seal on it – a Catholic England for ever. Be thankful she's barren.'

'How can I be thankful for another woman's barrenness, when I have two of my own in the nursery?' Agnes's daughter, another Elizabeth, had been born in May, Harry standing godfather. It was he who had pressed the parents to give their second daughter the same name as the first, as a compliment to the young Princess who waited at Hatfield to know her fate.

'Is it a time to bring children into such a world?' Harry asked her. 'Remember what things were done in Spain under Torquemada, and still are. It will be the same here, short of a miracle. Other persecutions were political – this comes from the brain and will of a fanatic.'

Sir Nicholas shook his head. 'I cannot think a daughter of my good old King can be so wanton cruel.'

'Your good old King, father, had five Carthusian priors and monks hanged, drawn and quartered at Reading, twenty years ago, because they refused to swear the Oath of Supremacy that declared him Head of the Church, and had his good friend Thomas More beheaded for the same offence. What would you say is the prime element of Tudor blood – mother's milk?'

'Well. Let it be. We must hope for the best, and behave ourselves like sensible folk.' He ambled out to the gardens, the big hound at his side.

'Father's words are brave, but even he feels the cold wind now,' Simon said. 'You were right to speak out to him, Hal.'

Jacquette was dancing.

Alone, in a seldom-used parlour in the most ancient part of the house, which had a floor of stout boards smooth to the feet, she was working out dance-steps to the tune of a galliard of which Sir Nicholas was particularly fond. One of his London guests had played it over and over at his request, so that Jacquette's quick ear had picked it up. She hummed it, moving gracefully, rapidly, pointing her feet, swaying and swirling, her scarlet taffeta skirts flying out and her hair tossing, and smiled as she danced, thinking of Sir Nicholas's pleasure at a new entertainment. Poor soul, he was not quite his exuberant self these days.

Gideon Baldwin, who had entered soundlessly, watched her from a shadowy corner. It was the first time he had been able to watch her alone, performing as it were only for his delight. Like a starving man at a table spread with rich food he gloated on her beauty; the lithe rounded limbs, the young bosom pushed up temptingly by the stiff corset, the white dimpled hands that were yet so strong. As she turned her head from side to side his eyes lingered on her face, that still seemed rounded like a child's, though she was a woman. There were tiny tucks of good humour at the corner of the full mouth, the colour of a pink rose, and the bloom of a ripe peach was on her soft cheeks, her eyes damson-dark. She was like an offering of fruit and flowers made to love's god.

He had not meant to speak today, but desire was too strong for him. 'Jacquette,' he said.

She paused in her dancing, startled, a hand to her heart. 'Who . . .? Oh. Master Baldwin.' Her tone was not welcoming.

'I was not spying on you,' he said. 'I heard you singing, and it drew me.'

'The dance is not ready to be seen,' she said stiffly. 'I would prefer to practise it alone.'

'You shall in a moment. But listen to me first. I never have you to myself, always in company, or with your . . . husband present. Let me have just this little time with you.' He left the dark corner and came towards her. She glanced hopefully at the open door, but there was no sign or sound of anyone in the corridor beyond it.

'So. What have you to say to me, Master Baldwin?'

'Have I any need to say it? Most beautiful Jacquette, you know I love you, you know my heart, soul and body are yours – I've seen the knowledge of it in your eyes, when they catch mine.' He was breathing quickly, a faint flush in his usually sallow cheeks. Jacquette's own were as scarlet as her kirtle.

'Indeed I do *not* know it, sir, or anything of the kind! What right have you to speak to me so, pray?'

'A lover's right – the right of one who worships you, one who claims you as his own.'

'How dare you! I belong to my husband and none beside – most certainly not to you.'

'Your husband.' Gideon's mouth twisted in scorn. 'That long-faced mountebank, an alehouse wayside hedge-and-ditch juggler kept on a rich man's charity and set up for better than he is. He has even lost his mirth, if he ever had any . . . What use is he to you, Jacquette, you, silk to his fustian?' His voice quickened. 'You hear how I talk now, that have always been silent before you? Have I not a way with words? With you I could do anything, be anything, not a miserable clerk to a stupid master. Only give yourself to me and you shall see.' He was advancing on her, she backing away. There was a small cabinet behind her – she glanced at it, looking for some kind of weapon, but there was only a small box on it, of ebony with corners of wrought steel. She snatched at it and held it in front of her, ready to strike him. He smiled.

'That toy will not daunt me, you know.

> "Desire
> Like fire
> Doth still aspire."

Did you ever learn that rhyme? I can teach you desire, Jacquette, such as I dare swear you've never felt yet, so hot that the hardest frost melts before it . . . Will you melt for me, Jacquette?'

His hands were on her waist now, holding her so close to him that she could not raise the hand that gripped the box. His face and voice were charged with lust; no longer Sir Nicholas's tight-lipped clerk, but a satyr. 'I had not meant to woo you like this . . . I had meant – but no matter for that, you are too much for me – your beauty, your woman's body, so soft . . .' His mouth came down on hers, urgent, cruel, devouring, stopping her gasped protests. He lifted it to whisper, his breath hot in her ear, 'I must have you, now, I must.'

She was being pressed up against the wall, forced by his body and by hands that were even stronger than her own. The box had dropped to the floor. The hands were wrenching, now at her kirtle, now at her bodice.

Jerking her head aside, away from his pursuing mouth, she screamed, a loud scream from lungs that were trained to project her voice. It startled him, so that he relaxed his grip on her, and she screamed again.

Outside the old wing of the house ran a path that was a short cut to the stables. Harry Brome, like the others, often used it in dry weather, as he was doing now. The scream, even heard through the closed garden door, stopped him in his tracks. He unlatched the door and went swiftly in.

Jacquette saw him first, and at her face of joyful relief Gideon turned. The two men confronted each other, the clerk in a fury of frustration, Harry grim, his hand on his sword.

'Baldwin was annoying you, mistress?' He knew it was an understatement. She nodded violently, unable to speak. Harry turned to Baldwin.

'Away with you, or take a beating. Out of my sight!'

The clerk's face was now as livid-pale as it had been flushed with passion. He moved to the door and there paused, his eyes fixed on Jacquette.

'You'll be sorry for this work, mistress. When others hear what I have to tell, it will please me very greatly to see you weep.'

XV
Unholy Vespers

Jacquette put up her hands to her disordered hair, smoothed down her skirts, and shook herself like a ruffled cat. Harry anticipated tears, perhaps a swoon. Instead she stood, hands on hips like a young fishwife, and uttered a stream of vehement French. Then she drew a deep breath, exhaled it, and smiled at him.

'Excuse me, sir. It is not polite to speak in French to an English person, I know. But then what I feel about that *crapaud* is not polite, and I do not know the English words for all of it. Now I feel better.' She sank before him in a deep curtsey which would have graced a court.

'I thank you with all my heart, sir, for your rescue of me. That creature would have ravished me in a moment.'

'Then I should have been mournfully obliged to kill him, madam. So we have both been spared – you from ravishment and I from murder. It was a blessed providence that I took the little path to the stables today, instead of the courtyard way.'

'Yes.' Calmer now, she looked at her rescuer as though she had never seen him before; he made a gallant figure, in his best attire today, velvet doublet, gold-buttoned, breeches of fine leather dyed a deep brown, and silk hose coloured cream. The fashionable flat cap, of brown velvet, sat aslant on curls the colour of sunset, a jewel winking in it. The jewel fascinated Jacquette. Was it blue or green, or iridescent? But there was no doubt about his eyes, a clear, true blue, not Tudor eyes at all, but Harry Brome's own.

She was not aware of staring at him, or that he was staring at her. It seemed natural and right that time had suspended itself while they viewed each other, for the first time, as man and woman. He had always thought her looks charming, for she was a little like his lost love, Joan; but Joan had been fragile, bird-boned, and this girl was slenderly robust, one of earth's daughters, life beating strong within her. The atmosphere of sexual struggle was still about her, creating an excitement Harry had not felt for too long.

Since Joan's death he had kept himself from women as far as possible, deeply afraid of condemning any to the same death, which in his mind had become one with birth. There had been a few easy wenches, who knew how not to produce bastard children. There was a middle-aged widow of ample charms in Oxford, who possessed wit and understanding as well as physical lure; she was always happy to see him, and he her, but there were no ties, and no vows.

And now there was another woman; not his father's paid servant the Merrymaid, but a girl of radiant loveliness in whose dark eyes he felt himself drowning. He forgot her husband, whose very existence had always distanced her from him as a matter of honour. In the room, in the world, were only themselves.

He half-whispered words he had often heard her sing, to her own pavane measure.

> *' "Belle qui tiens ma vie*
> *Captive dans tes yeux . . ." '*

Jacquette nodded. It was quite clear to her what had happened; she had her hungers too. Frankly, freely, she stood on tiptoe and put her arms round his neck, offering her mouth for a kiss that was like no other she had ever given or taken – Alan's gentle kisses (so rare now), the daring salutes of Sir Nicholas's gallant friends, the savage assault by Gideon Baldwin. There was no time or place or memory: only a delirious joy and sweetness.

Harry drew away from her at last, shaken and breathing fast.

'A reward for my noble rescuer,' Jacquette said. He searched her face for mockery, but there was none. She had said the right thing, words that covered the situation, from which they could both now withdraw with honour.

He said, 'I was going to ride. Will you ride with me? The air is clear as crystal today.'

It was indeed one of those golden days September can give, a warm sun shining and a light breeze blowing, Oxfordshire basking like an animal in this, the last glorious weather at the end of a grey, cloudy English summer. On the hills above them bracken was glowing coppery-brown, and trees turning gold in the slow lovely death of their leaves. By the river boys were fishing. A kingfisher flew up before them in a vivid flash of blue, something silver wriggling in its beak. The two horses moved unhurriedly, feeling their riders at leisure; Harry's big chestnut mare Amabel, and Jacquette's Blaise, older and slower than when he had carried her in her days of travel, a horse of gentle nature who had led, since his coming to Brome Court, a completely happy life.

The two who rode spoke little; there was no need. Jacquette remarked that since sheep were not white at all, but a sort of dingy cream, it was surprising that they were always called white, and Harry agreed that this was so. He added that it was an unusually good year for apples, so there would be a great cider-making soon.

Little else was said before they turned homewards, but for Jacquette asking, 'Did you write your English play?' and Harry answering, 'No, but now I shall.'

They parted in the stable-yard like courteous acquaintances, and went back to their own lives and places, equally bemused. Nobody, nobody at all, Jacquette resolved, should ever know what had happened on that fateful morning, least of all Alan, whose melancholy would not be at all benefited by the knowledge that his wife had just fallen violently in love with someone else.

Gideon Baldwin timed his revenge, very carefully, for the Sunday evening service held in the Brome family chapel. Once they had called it Evensong, now it was Vespers, to the great satisfaction of the Reverend Father Jackson, Sir Nicholas's detested jackanapes. By custom, everyone who could move at all was present, even the boy who looked after the pigs and was only, as the saying went, ninepence to the shilling. Father Jackson had exempted Nick and his baby sister and their nurse from attending, for his own sake, since Nick's dislike of sitting still was only equalled by the loudness of his voice, and babies were a notorious nuisance in church. Otherwise, the chapel was full, the servants standing, only the family and Dorothy being accommodated with seats. Alan and Jacquette stood together, in the front rank of the congregation.

The last '*In nomine Patris . . .*' had been intoned, the last 'Amen' chorused, and the tired servants were thinking longingly of their beds, when Gideon, who had as usual been assisting Father Jackson, stepped forward and held up a hand.

'Sir Nicholas, my masters and mistresses, and you, friends, your pardon – I must speak to you on a grave matter.'

'God's blood, what is it now, man?' roared Sir Nicholas. 'The service is done.'

'Again, your pardon, sir. But in the name of truth and justice I cannot keep silent longer.'

Everyone looked round-eyed at everyone else in the dramatic pause. Then he pointed a finger directly at Jacquette and Alan.

'I denounce those two persons, Alan Thornwood and Jacquette Thornwood, so-called, of deceiving their master most wickedly, of being concerned in criminal pursuits, and of the damned sin of fornication. Know, good people, that they are not man and wife.'

A general gasp went through the chapel like a rushing wind. Jacquette and Alan stared wildly at one another.

'I have spent time and money,' Gideon continued, 'money that my kind master gave me for my own use, in assuring myself that what I had heard a whisper of was indeed true. I have travelled up and down the countryside, I have spoken with thieves and harlots, I have gone cheek by jowl with men of impious life –'

Sir Nicholas's face had turned from its normal healthy pink to a flaring crimson. He shouted, 'By Cock, speak out, man, if thou must, or I'll come up there and fell thee!'

'Patience, sir, I draw to it. I met at last with a woman who had been this man's doxy or mort, as they call it in their cant, and had done him many kindnesses when they travelled the roads performing tricks and mummeries for money. She was in hopes he would marry her, for even the lowest of this kind long to be made honest women, but to her great grief he left their troupe, or tribe, and went travelling alone.

'When next she met with him he was no more alone, for he

had seduced or ravished a young maid and taken her from her guardian's house.'

At Jacquette's indignant outcry Alan gripped her wrist painfully tight, whispering, 'Hear him out.'

'With this wench he came to the camp where the tribe had halted to ask their *patrico* to join them in marriage. Now a *patrico* is one who lives by marrying vagrants, or pretending to marry them, for mostly *patricos* have never been ordained, nor was this man, a drunken rogue who muttered words over them and took his fee. And the woman, who told me this, told me also that the false bride was not well-born, but had been a vagrant in her childhood, a French stroller, whom a benevolent gentlewoman saved from a life of harlotry.'

At which point the speaker encountered Harry's furious eyes, and began to gabble the rest of his denunciation. 'Furthermore, this pretty pair was imprisoned in the county of Surrey, and the man known to be in possession of stolen gold; and furthermore –'

Harry pushed back his chair with a loud scraping sound, and marched up to Gideon, whose arm he took in a powerful grip.

'Furthermore, you will not speak of a lady in her presence, or make any more accusations until those you accuse have spoken for themselves. Master Thornwood, come forward and make your case.'

'Well said, Hal,' Sir Nicholas cried. To a murmur of mingled conjecture, amazement, and plain avid interest, Alan left Jacquette's side and joined Harry by the altar. He was ghost-pale and trembling with shock, and paused to draw a deep breath before he could trust himself to speak. Jacquette, furious as she was, watched him with a deep concern and pity, willing him to be calm and convincing.

In a voice that those at the back had to strain to hear, he said, 'This man has spoken evil of me and my wife. For she is my wife, despite what he says. The *patrico* may have been no true priest, but we were hand-fasted before witnesses, and that is a recognised marriage.'

'Not by the Church!' cried Father Jackson. 'In Roman law the *usus*, yes, but by the *Lex Ecclesiae* –'

'The *Lex Ecclesiae* is not in question,' Harry interposed. 'A hand-fasting union may be binding, all know that. Continue, Master Thornwood.'

Alan was swaying on his feet, his eyes opening and shutting. Harry saw that he was fainting, and caught him before he fell, laying him gently down on the altar-step. Jacquette ran forward and knelt at his side, feeling his hands, his cheek, his heart, and looking wildly up at Harry.

'Only a swoon,' he told her. 'He'll recover in a moment.'

She leapt to her feet and faced the staring, murmuring household.

'Master Thornwood did not seduce or ravish me!' she told them, her voice ringing back from the farthest wall. 'It was I who led him into taking me with him – I left my guardian's house of my own free will. And she did *not* save me from harlotry –I was never a vagrant, but a *jongleuse*, of a family who come down from the *trouvères*, the lords of minstrelsy!'

Harry's smile encouraged her. 'It is true we were in prison, but it was for a foolish doctor's mistake, not for a crime. And yes, we did carry gold, twenty gold pieces, which my father left hidden for me before he died. As for the woman this man talked with, she was never betrothed to my husband, but she hated and envied me very much and set on me to murder me. See!' She pulled the hair away from her brow. 'This scar, it is how he traced this woman, this devil – he asked me of it one day and I told him it was her knife made it.'

As she paused for breath Harry said quietly, 'Tell them about the other morning.'

She nodded. 'If any asks why this man has spoken against us, it is not in the name of truth and justice, but because he hates us. He would have ravished me and was prevented.' She was not going to bring Harry's name into it. 'Now you have heard the truth, and you must judge.'

Her head drooped against Harry's shoulder as he led her to his father's side, to such a murmuring as the chapel had never before heard. Sir Nicholas took her from his son, embraced her, and gave her a hearty kiss. Simon and Agnes came forward and did the same, and Harry, after a second's hesitation, kissed her hand.

Alan, sitting up now, watched with a faint smile, proud of her. Gideon sat with a stony glare.

The women had clustered round Jacquette, Agnes and Dorothy closest, the others as near as they could get, since she was now a household heroine. At Sir Nicholas's kiss she had begun to weep, and seemed unable to stop. Agnes whispered, 'Be brave, be merry, all believed you – he has done no harm. When we go upstairs you shall nurse Elizabeth and have some of Simon's Gascon wine.'

Sir Nicholas advanced on his clerk. 'You spoke ill. You have an ill mind. I do not like evil men within my household. It's said your father was a priest and you a bastard; I can believe both, you snivelling feigner. This is a good house – get from it now before I forget myself and kick you before me like a football.'

Gideon was utterly confounded. He had cunning, book-learning, eloquence, but he was in all other ways stupid. To him, the outcome of his researches into the Thornwoods' history, and his neat twisting of the facts, could only have meant complete triumph for him and defeat and dismissal for them. Instead the reverse had happened. He had lost his employment, his home, his local reputation, and all the money he had spent in tracing the Hooders, and he had also lost all hope of gaining Jacquette, who had been the reason for it all. Once the two of them were discredited, his reasoning had run, he would have stepped nobly forward and offered to marry Jacquette, that fallen woman, now it was proved that she was free to wed. Cursèd bitch! If she had only given in to him when he was rash enough to essay her he might have been satisfied and have abandoned his plan for the confrontation.

'You are losing a good clerk,' was all he could say to Sir Nicholas, who replied, 'There are others – honest ones. Go with my man Martin to the counting-house and you shall have what's owing to you. And,' he shouted after the clerk's retreating back, 'may the devil go with you!'

XVI

O true love have you my gold?

The iron bell that hung by the door of Brome Court's great hall clanged once, twice. Then, not being answered, it rang impatiently again and again, until a serving-man ran to open the door.

Father Jackson waited on the steps. In the courtyard a stocky man, drably dressed, was tethering two horses to a post.

'I would speak with Sir Nicholas,' the priest snapped.

'He is not within, sir, but gone hunting.'

This not surprising answer brought a frown to Jackson's brow. 'I will wait.' He strode past the servant and took a seat by the fire, warming his thin shanks, first one, then the other. And there he might have sat all day, but for a sudden deluge of rain that brought Sir Nicholas home prematurely from his sport. He was wet, foiled of his hare, and not pleased to see his visitor.

'What, is it Sunday again, or are we to have an extra mass?'

'No, sir. I am here on a different matter. I have come with a warrant to arrest the person of your servant Alan Thornwood.'

Sir Nicholas's eyes popped. 'Arrest – you? Have you been appointed Constable, then? Only the Watch have licence to arrest.'

'An officer of the Watch waits outside, sir.'

'Make yourself plain, man. You say you are come, or this officer is come, to arrest my minstrel Alan. Upon what charge? You heard him with your own ears refute that gallimaufry of rubbish my clerk threw at him. He was innocent of all of it, as even you must acknowledge, and there's an end to it. Will you now tell me he once stole a toy from a babe, and must be tried for it?' The priest did not smile.

'He must be tried, sir, but not for that. My warrant is from the Church Court, who would examine him on a charge of heresy.'

'Heresy? *Heresy?* Are your brains turned?'

Silently Jackson unrolled a paper and handed it over. Sir Nicholas was not a quick reader, and the crabbed writing only served to make him angrier. He seized the handbell used to summon servants and rang it violently, shouting, 'Here's a madman! Some of you, come and pitch him out neck and crop. Luke, Martin, to me, I say!'

The men were in the room almost as he spoke, alerted by his tone and eager to throw out the unpopular Jackson, but he repelled them with a stern look, the one he reserved for admonishing sinners in church.

'Sir Nicholas, I advise you to not resist this warrant, for it is a true one and made by the general order of the Queen. The Court has learned of things that make the man Thornwood a notable suspect, and he must be questioned. If your servants do me violence it will make no odds – the warrant will still hold. Call in the officer if you disbelieve me.'

Sir Nicholas did not disbelieve him. Serious trouble could come from tangling with the law, either civil or ecclesiastical, especially these days. He ordered Martin to find Alan and fetch him to the hall.

Alan told the horrified Jacquette, 'I knew it. I saw it in the cards long ago, but not what form it would take. I am to be tried.'

'No! There is some dreadful error. Go, go out by the little door and hide in the gardens or the stables. *I* will answer for you, they will listen to me. That Gideon Baldwin is behind this, mark me! Well, I know what I know of him.'

'I'm still man enough to speak up for myself.' Alan detached himself from her clinging arms. 'I tell you, it must be.' Anxiously she hurried after him and Martin to the hall.

Jackson read out the warrant, tonelessly, impersonally. Then Alan said, 'Very well. I will go with you. Where do you take me?'

'To Reading.'

Jacquette cried, 'No!', then, 'I will go with him.'

'You are not summoned, mistress, and the Court sits in private.' Desperately she wished for Harry to appear, Harry who had saved her once, who could save Alan, surely. But Harry had ridden to Henley on farm business, and today could not be her angel. She looked helplessly from the priest to Sir Nicholas, who seethed with impotent rage, pacing the room. He swung round to Jackson.

'That poxy clerk of mine has made more accusations, isn't that so? Aye, I see it in your face. Well, when you come to Reading you may tell your cursèd Court and that lozel, that scroyle, that prating, lying, brothel-hatched son of a neighing assinego that I'll have his neck for this, marry that I will, by God's Blood and the nightcap of St Peter. Tell him that, tell him that!'

'I would have a care of what you say, sir,' put in Jackson primly, 'or you may be the next to have a warrant out for your arrest – for blasphemy at the very least.' From a window he beckoned the officer, who, impatient with waiting, hurried in. 'Where's my prisoner, your reverence?'

'There he is, take him.'

But Alan said with dignity. 'I'll go without holding. Only send someone to fetch my cloak and cap. It's an ill day for riding half-clad. Not you, wife – a servant will fetch them.' Jacquette clung to him. He kissed her and stroked her disordered hair, holding close. So that only she could hear, he said:

' "Oh true love have you my gold,
And can you set me free?
Or are you come to see me hung
All on the gallows tree?" '

In the song the answer should be, 'Yes, I've brought thy gold'; but she could not give it, or any kind of assurance. No assurance, no promise, no comfort. She said lamely, 'You will be back soon, I know it.'

She watched him go from the window, riding a horse brought round from the stables; Ned had died two years earlier. The priest and the officer rode on either side. At the end of the drive Alan turned and waved, with a last long look at the house.

Sir Nicholas watched too, standing behind her. When the sorry cavalcade was out of sight he went to his fireside chair and slumped into it. 'Damn 'em,' he said, 'damn 'em to eternity, for taking my minstrel.' Then, speaking in ordinary measured tones, he launched into such a stream of blasphemy as Jacquette had never heard from any lips. Beside it her mild outburst to Harry was nothing. Imprecations concerning the anatomy of various holy personages flowed from him, country oaths so crude that he would not normally have uttered them in public, let alone before a woman, curses and threats that were terrible to hear.

Jacquette filled a goblet from wine that had been put on the table by one of the serving-men, and gave it to Sir Nicholas. He gulped it down and held out the cup for another, which received the same treatment. His face was crimson and red capillaries threaded the whites of his eyes. Suddenly he flung the goblet away from him and before it had rolled as far as the hearth was out of the room. Jacquette heard him bellowing his way along the corridor that led to the domestic quarters. She sat down in the chair he had vacated and put her head in her hands.

She had fallen into a kind of doze or dream, and Dorothy was shaking her.

'What's to do, Jacquette? What's all the pother? I heard a fearful commotion when I was up in the nurseries, but the nurse was at her dinner and I couldn't leave Elizabeth. Are you ill, child? What ails you, and where's Sir Nicholas?'

Dully, Jacquette told her what had happened. The housekeeper wrung her hands.

'Oh Lord, oh my dear soul, here's a parlous piece of work, and just as all seemed righted after that unseemliness in the chapel. Surely there's some error, or some malice that will be found out?'

'Malice, indeed, dame. But I could not stop it, or Sir Nicholas, nor anyone. Alan is gone to Reading with them.'

Dorothy, nervously plucking at her apron, hurried to the rain-streaked window. 'A horseman – perhaps Sir Nicholas – no, Harry. Now we shall hear some sense.'

Harry strode into the hall, his cloak dripping and his boots sodden, hair dark with rain. 'Where's my father? Luke has some tale –'

'A true one.' Again Jacquette told the story. Harry frowned deeply. 'I must speak to my father. But where is he? No one has seen him.'

'He may be at dinner by now,' Dorothy suggested eagerly. 'I'll go see.'

'I looked in a moment since and he was not there. The stables! They will know . . .'

The head groom pulled his forelock. 'Sir, he went off in a tearing rush, as though he were mad. I couldn't tell much he said or reason wi' him, for he paid no heed but up and galloped off.'

Harry looked beyond him, into the shadowy stable. 'But Casimir is still there! What mount did he take? Not Brutus?'

'Aye, sir. Brutus was saddled and Sir Nicholas took him, will I, nill I.'

'But you know he was unfit to be ridden, at least by a man as heavy as my father! He's only lately broken, and jibs at much weight on his back. Did I not tell you, all of you, that only George was permitted to ride him?'

'Aye, you did, Master Harry, and George had him out for a trot this morning, but Sir Nicholas wouldn't be told, and wouldn't be told.' The groom was almost weeping. They all knew well that the young master's temper could match the old one's.

'Why the devil was Brutus saddled? Never mind, never mind. Did my father say nothing at all of where he was going?'

'Only . . . he spoke very confused and mazedly, but I think 'twas – Reading.'

Four men rode through the steady downpour; Harry, the young groom George, and Sir Nicholas's body-servants, Martin and Luke. If Sir Nicholas had run into trouble with the mettlesome Brutus George would change horses with him. Any stable recriminations would keep. Harry was wet through, hungry, deeply disturbed by Alan's arrest, but his present concern was for his father's safety. To go cantering off to Reading, with no notion of how it could help Alan, was a piece of wild chivalry all too characteristic of Sir Nicholas. They must catch him before he reached Reading, or he would get himself into fearful trouble with the authorities; worse trouble, probably, than Alan was in already, for Baldwin owed him a deep grudge.

Harry tried to exercise his mind in the remembering of lines from Terence, whose comedy might relieve his gloom, if only slightly. A line came into his head: '*Adprime in vita esse utile, ut nequid nimis*' – the most important thing in life is never to have too much of anything. He smiled wryly, seeing an aptness in it to the present situation.

A jagged fork of lightning split the leaden skies, and a crack of thunder. It was only a little past noon, yet as dark as mid-evening, and the rough road was dissolving into mud and loose stones, difficult for the horses' footing. How much further – five miles, six? Sir Nicholas must have made a good pace, fury lending him wings . . . or lending Brutus wings . . .

'Master Harry.' Martin's voice broke into his thought. 'I think I see something – yonder, beyond that post.'

The post was all that remained of a wayside shrine, destroyed in Henry's reign and not yet rebuilt. Half of a weeping Magdalene and a few carved fragments of robes remained. Almost at its foot, sprawled on the ground in the wet long grass, lay Sir Nicholas. He would never move again, for his neck had snapped when the horse threw him.

Three riders halted under the walls of Greyfriars Church in Reading. Rain fell relentlessly on their already soaked garments and splashed into the pools it had made round the ancient headstones in the churchyard. Alan was somewhat uncharitably glad that his two escorts were as wet as he was, but it had not improved their tempers. Told curtly to dismount, he was seized by the officer and unceremoniously jerked towards a building a few yards from the church which seemed at one time to have been part of it, as its lancet windows and a few defaced statues in niches testified. At the door Father Jackson left them, saying to Alan with grim satisfaction, 'I will see you again when the Court sits.'

The officer, without a word, pushed his prisoner inside. The building had evidently been part of a monastery in its time, there were cells leading off a flintstone corridor, and remains of chapels, altered from their original purpose. The officer opened a heavy door, glanced in and shut it again; Alan glimpsed several people inside, an old man, a woman and small child, and a haggard face that might have belonged to man or woman. Then he found himself thrust into one of the cells so roughly that he staggered. Before he could ask the man any questions the door was shut and noisily locked.

The cell was bare except for straw on its floor, exceedingly filthy, and something which might have been intended for a straw pallet. The smell of the place was noisome, sickening, though fresh air came from a small unglazed window with two bars across it. Alan leaned against the wall, unwilling to sit on the foul floor. He wondered how long he would have to endure imprisonment before his trial. He wondered if he would ever see Jacquette again. The glimpse of his future given him by the cards had shown him arrest and imprisonment, but nothing further. Perhaps there was nothing further, for time seemed to have stopped.

He surveyed the window. It was big enough for a slender agile person to get through, but for its stout bars. Outside it was grass, dotted with small headstones, perhaps the graves of monks who had inhabited the place, and beyond a building with no visible windows, the back of a tall old house. Beside it ran a narrow alley.

Alan put his hand between the bars, pressing close to the aperture for the sake of the air it admitted, though the cell was cold enough to chill the bones. Rain filled his upturned palm; he thought of it as the tears of heaven.

The passing-bell had ceased to toll for Sir Nicholas. Now he lay in the family vault beneath the floor of the parish church, while the Great Hall of his house hummed with the voices of more than a hundred guests at his funeral-feast. Distant relatives, the neighbouring gentry, farmers and shepherds, cottagers and innkeepers, had all crowded in to drink wine boiled with sugar and cinnamon and eat rich fare. A good many dogs had invited themselves to the feast, and were enjoying bones and scraps under the feet of the guests.

Dorothy, who had at last subsided into a chair at the head of one of the long tables, let out her breath with relief that it was all over but for the monumental clearing-up, which would not be her responsibility.

And it had all gone so well. It had fallen to her to carry out the duties of a housewife on such occasions, and they had all been fulfilled. Mourning-clothes had been got together for herself, the family and the servants: fortunately nearly everyone who had been in the house when Lady Brome died had kept some black garments laid away, still serviceable even if out of fashion. She was pleased with hers, a gown with a slimming line to it and an extremely becoming English hood with an edging of pearls. It was a comfort to know that she looked better in her mourning than in the bright colours she preferred, being still buxom and bonny of complexion.

Then there had been (she ticked them off on her fingers) the making of Sir Nicholas's linen shroud and the ordering of the coffin, the painting of a hatchment to hang first over the door of the house, then in the church, the buying of mourning-rings and gloves to give as memorial presents to relatives and close friends, gifts of money to be taken round to the neighbouring poor . . . there seemed to be no end to it, and all packed within five days, during which folk had come from near and far to pay their respects to the corpse, laid out in state.

Dorothy glanced round the room to make sure that none of the servants was making too free with the wine. If the guests did, that was their privilege, and could always be excused as arising from extremity of grief, but the dead man's own household must behave soberly. The children were getting somewhat out of hand; the youngest child of Meg, Sir Nicholas's daughter, had just been sick over somebody's gown, and was being hustled out, and Nick would certainly follow his cousin's example later, for he was helping himself freely from the dishes. On the whole, it was a happy party. How Sir Nicholas himself would have enjoyed it, and what a pity he could not be there! She would never believe his soul was now in Purgatory, as Father Jackson said, for who would keep such a jolly innocent in pain for a few thousand years?

Dorothy absent-mindedly poured herself another cup of wine, on top of the seven or eight she had already drunk, and a tear rolled down her cheek. If only he could have brought himself to marry her she would have been making the funeral arrangements in her proper capacity as widow. And now she would be My Lady.

Another tear fell. A hand stole round her head-dress and gently wiped the tear away. 'What, sweeting? never weep.' It was the voice of Giles Buckle, a well-to-do farmer from the other side of Henley, who had been a hunting and drinking-crony of Sir Nicholas. He was a large, comfortable man, himself still in mourning for his wife, and disliking the garb as much as most people did. He too had taken more than a few cups of the excellent wine, and was feeling expansive, after the dolour of the grave-side. He had always had an eye to his friend's ripe comely mistress, but honour had kept him at a decent and proper distance; this was the first time he had got an arm round her pleasantly-billowing shoulders. Her grateful smile emboldened him to plant a hearty buss on her cheek, at which she blushed and dimpled. Giles Buckle drew up a stool beside her; they began to murmur.

Harry Brome was not enjoying the funeral feast. He was Sir Henry now, the new baronet, and handsomer in his sable suit than any man there. But the loss of his father grieved him greatly, and the silly needless manner of it. If George had not been at dinner – if the head groom had refused to let Brutus out – most of all, if that knave of a priest had not arrested Alan. It had not only been choler that had sent Sir Nicholas off on that fatal ride, but the shock to his feudal soul that hands should have been laid on one of his own people, under his protection.

Not Brutus's fault, poor beast. He had been caught a mile away, running aimlessly round with his reins dangling, and brought back by George to his stable, where his nervous temperament would be allowed to settle before he was ridden abroad again.

Five days since, Alan had been taken away. During that time Harry had not had a moment to spare from the funeral arrangements. Jacquette had ridden to Reading with a servant and found out the prison at Greyfriars, but they had refused her admission. The Court hearing, they said, had not yet taken place. Word would be sent to Brome Court when it had. She had come back infinitely dejected, as she looked now, drooping on a window-seat, her head turned away from the room.

I will help you, my sweet, pretty lady, Harry silently promised her. Tomorrow I shall ride to Reading, and any man who keeps me out of that prison shall feel the weight of my hand. Even perhaps, the point of my sword.

XVII
Of Reading Gaol

The Church Court was in session.

At one end of the panelled enclosure the judge, priest-vicar of the largest parish of Reading, sat on his raised throne, beneath a canopy carved with escutcheons. He looked down on a large table, at which the witnesses sat. Today there were only two, Gideon Baldwin and Father Jackson. A notary sat at a desk, his paper and pens before him, and along one side of the table five men in black robes, two magistrates and three priests called together to judge the prisoner's case.

The prisoner, Alan Thornwood, stood at the end of the Court, facing the judge. They had not bound his hands, since he was not yet convicted. He was bearded, louse-bitten and filthy. He had hardly slept since his arrest, prevented by cold, discomfort, hunger and the noises of the prison – cries, moans and some drunken laughter. It was hard to stand upright, weak as he was after six days of stale water and mouldy bread, but he found the strength to bear himself well and face the judge steadfastly.

The Oath was administered. It was a newly-designed one, in which the prisoner affirmed his loyalty to the Queen and the Church. Then the Apparitor, a magistrate, whose view of ecclesiastical matters was supposed to be impersonal and fair, began the questions.

'You stand accused of unlawfully administering the sacrament of baptism to an infant according to the late Book of Common Prayer, now prohibited and altogether proscribed and abolished, its use forbidden on pain of grave punishment. This offence was allegedly committed on the twenty-second day of August, Anno Domini 1554. Do you plead guilty or not guilty?'

'I . . . it is true that I . . .'

'Guilty or not guilty?'

'Guilty.'

'You furthermore administered the sacrament in defiance of one present who was prepared to do so according to the Latin Missal, as laid down to be used in all churches and public places of worship.' The Apparitor glanced at Gideon Baldwin, who said, 'This is true. I had begun to read the service from the Missal, but it was taken from my hand.'

'Your reason for this, prisoner?'

'My master, or his son – I forget which – wished the service to be in English. The Queen had not yet been proclaimed, and the English service was lawful.'

'And why were you in particular chosen?'

Alan hesitated. 'I think – it was because I can read well and quickly. The child was dying, it was necessary to baptise in haste.'

'In such a house you were the only person who could read?'

'No. But . . .'

The Apparitor addressed the judge. 'These answers are not satisfactory. I have it on record that there were several persons present of the Brome family, whom we may take to be lettered, even the women. Father Jackson, is this true?'

'I cannot say,' answered the priest sourly. 'But to my mind the whole family was tainted with Protestantism, unwilling to hear mass more than once a day – an ungodly household. They should be arraigned along with this man.'

'Write, notary. Who is the head of the household, Father?'

'At the time of the unlawful baptism it was Sir Nicholas Brome, but he is suddenly dead, and Sir Henry succeeds.'

Alan started with shock. Sir Nicholas dead! His mind raced through the possible reasons. Was it good or bad for his cause, that Harry Brome was now lord of Brome Court? Sharply intuitive in his recent state of melancholy, Alan had sensed the new strong attraction between Harry and Jacquette; perhaps Harry would be glad to have him removed. He put away the idea as being shameful and unworthy.

Gideon, too, was startled, and cast down, for he had hoped to involve Sir Nicholas, who had dismissed him and cost him his livelihood. But he hated Harry too, for robbing him of his conquest of Jacquette; perhaps he would serve instead.

He was to be disappointed. The courts were reluctant to condemn the 'better sort' of people, unless they were clerics. The poor and humble might be made into examples without repercussions, but the rich might give trouble, and were in any case good at talking themselves out of things. The prisoner before them today was a poor minstrel, well-spoken and not ignorant, but fair game for strict questioning.

Father Jackson said peevishly, 'There was no call for anyone but myself to baptise the infant, yet I was not sent for.'

'There was no time, the babe was dying.'

'Silence!' The judge banged on the table before him. 'The prisoner will answer when questioned, not otherwise.'

One of the other priests spoke up, mildly. 'It is not better to baptise a child by the most simple rite, even if a lay person must officiate, rather than send its soul to Limbo?'

'The rite was not simple, Father,' retorted Jackson, 'it was the baptismal service of the English Church.'

The Apparitor was getting tired of discussions that got nowhere. 'There is another charge brought by Master Baldwin,' he said. 'Read it, notary.'

' "That being a person of evil life, having lived carnally with a woman whom he had vilely seduced and to whom he was not lawfully wed, he was in the County of Surrey apprehended for blasphemy and cast into prison, from which he suddenly escaped and fled." '

'How answer you, prisoner?'

Managing to contain his anger at being once again charged by Gideon's testimony of crimes never committed, Alan answered, 'My wife and I are lawfully wed according to the custom of hand-fasting, and in the town of Dorking I was imprisoned on the word of a crackbrained doctor, and the charge was not blasphemy but the use of Latin charms. He was a fanatical Protestant who hated all popery.'

'Ah, you call it popery,' one of the priests said swiftly.

'I call it what he called it.'

'These Latin charms,' said the Apparitor, 'what were they?'

'Harmless. Old rhymes against a superflux of blood.'

'Recite one.'

Alan's brain was as starved as his body. All memory of the words left him; he stared blankly at the Apparitor.

'You use such "charms" in the tricks you perform as part of your trade, do you not?'

Not one word of Latin came into Alan's mind. With the dim idea that he was being asked for the sort of gibberish he and Jacquette used in conjuring acts, he said mechanically, *'Droch myroch, senaroth betu baroch assmanoth, rousee farounsee, hey passe passe.'*

All present hastily crossed themselves. 'Devil's names!' Father Jackson cried. 'This is no Latin, but witchcraft – we have a sorcerer here! *Vade me retro, Sathanas!'*

'Is it so, you use sorcery?' the Apparitor flung at Alan.

'No! I would never . . . these are but silly made-up words to fool people. Not true words at all.'

'Not true words indeed, but false, wicked ones, unfit for Christian ears. This man is dangerous, masters.'

The notary spoke up. 'There is something here in the charge alleged by Master Baldwin – that the prisoner used divination and communion with spirits in the exercise of his trade.'

The Apparitor searched his manuscript. 'It is so. Can you say more of that, Master Baldwin?'

'The prisoner was known to foretell the future from the reading of playing-cards and other symbols, and one of the household told me that he was not as other men but born with an unholy faculty, to speak with spirits and devils, who told him things that should be hidden. I know, for instance that he keeps in his bedchamber a female devil or succubus, which has carnal knowledge of him nightly and whispers to him unholy words.'

'No!' said Alan wildly. 'No such thing. I have a sort of sixth sense, as many have, to see a little way beyond the present. My mother had it. It is nothing evil and I would never make bad use of it. I know nothing of spirits and devils, I swear it by this –' He pulled out the crucifix hidden by his collar and put it to his lips.

The Apparitor shook his head. 'What say you to that, Father Jackson?'

'That the Evil One may quote Scripture and the ungodly carry a crucifix.'

'My mother put that cross round my neck when I was a little child,' Alan said. 'I swear on her memory that I use no magic.'

After some whispering the Apparitor sat down and Father Jackson rose, with an inclination to the judge. 'Prisoner, tell the Court your beliefs as to Transsubstantiation.'

'I don't know what that is, Father.'

'It is the word used by the Holy Catholic Church to express her teaching on the conversion of the Bread and Wine of the Eucharist into the Body and Blood of Christ. Do you truly and solemnly swear that you believe this, that no morsel of the substance of the Bread and Wine remains in the Eucharist, but only His precious Body and Blood?'

The question was half-gabbled, being one Father Jackson had asked often before. Alan failed to take it in. It was not a problem he had ever considered deeply. 'The Bread is the Body,' he said, faltering, 'the Wine is the Blood.'

'Ah, but in whole substance? What do you say to the point of "outward appearance", eh?'

'I can't say, sir. I can't think clear.'

There followed a rapid fire of involved questions on doctrine and belief which would have been above Alan's head at the best of times, and were at that moment incomprehensible. He shook his head wearily, not attempting to answer.

'You see?' Jackson turned to the judge in triumph. 'The devil will not let him speak lest he betray himself.'

'The man is ailing,' said the old priest who had spoken kindly before. 'Your questions were too harsh and came too quick, Father. May I ask them again, simply and clearly?'

'No,' Jackson snapped. 'They have been asked once and not answered. It is enough.'

Alan thought he heard condemnation in the last words, and looking from one to another of them, condemned himself out of his own mouth. 'How should I answer? I know no more of such matters than you do, whether the Bread is no more bread and the Wine no more wine, or any of these mysteries. All is words, words, words with you. I cannot understand them, any more than I understand why I was told two years ago that I must not worship as a Catholic, then told but a wink of an eye later that I must not worship as a Protestant. King Henry persecuted one, Queen Mary persecutes the other – I but call myself an honest Christian, and you'll tell me there is wrong in that, I doubt it not.'

A silence followed his rash words, a silence of utter agreement. None of them could doubt what they had heard. The Apparitor rose.

'Masters, there is but one conclusion. We have here a heretic of the foulest kind, and of such it is said "let him be Anathema".' He bowed to the judge. 'Your Worship, be pleased to pronounce sentence.'

The Brome family were at supper when a messenger from Father Jackson arrived with a letter. Harry read it, and turned as scarlet with shock and rage as his father might have done. He rose to his feet and banged the table for silence.

'Hear this, from our parish priest. "Your servant Alan Thornwood was this day questioned before the Ecclesiastical Court and by one consent deemed to be heretic. Seven days hence in the Market Place at Reading he is to die by fire." '

Jacquette would always remember that moment, and see everything in her mind's eye exactly as it was then: the candle-light shining back from some brass object hanging beside the hearth, the carving-knife in Dorothy's hand arrested in mid-air, where she sat at the foot of the table, the cold stare of a Brome ancestor from his portrait on the wall. She would always smell the rich sweet scent of hops newly picked, the savoury tang of roast meat lingering on the air, the heavy musky perfume with which Agnes saturated her clothes and herself.

Horror held others round the table in a clutch of silence. Then Jacquette slipped sideways from her stool in a faint.

When, after a few moments, the women brought her round, she began to babble in French, in a voice higher than her own, sometimes sobbing or shrieking. Dorothy, who had long experience of hysteria in maidservants, dealt a ringing slap to both her cheeks.

The shrieking ceased. She came out of her near-fit to find herself still on the ground, watched by a ring of grave faces. Agnes was weeping, Simon trying to comfort her. A cluster of servants had appeared and were whispering, among themselves, horror-struck.

Harry was bending over her, holding wine to her lips.

'Drink. Sit up if you can. So.' He gave her his hand and helped her to her feet, then turned to the others.

'I must talk with Jacquette alone about this dreadful business. Leave us, if you will.'

When all but themselves had gone Harry sat Jacquette in the armed chair that had been Sir Nicholas's. In it she looked small, shrunken, and as though she had aged ten years. Harry felt as though he had too, but the light of battle was in his eyes. He sat down opposite her, and sent out all the strength of his personality to catch and hold her attention while he spoke slowly, measuredly.

'Jacquette, we have just heard a most terrible thing. More terrible to you than any of us. I know, believe me, how you must feel at this moment.'

'No,' she whispered, 'no, impossible. You see, it is all my fault. It was I led him into this. And I did not love him enough . . .'

'Stuff,' said Harry briskly. 'You talk nonsense and I have no time to listen to it. Now hark to me. This is no time for tears or lamentations; they may come after. We must make a plan.' Leaning forward he took her hands in his and held them tightly, almost painfully. This was the plan he proposed.

The next morning, early, he and she would ride to Reading. They would visit Alan, and this time nobody would gainsay them. Harry well knew the value of a masterly manner and a good loud voice. They would take with them what comforts Alan would most need – blankets for warmth, wine and food, aqua-vitae, clean linen, and money with which to bribe the gaoler. Then they would visit every magistrate and priest in the town who might help, and use every persuasion known to man. If all failed Harry would ride to London and beg for an audience of the Queen. As he talked Jacquette felt the worst of the shock lightening, he was so full of confidence and authority. She had known, after all, that something like this might happen, from the moment Alan was arrested, and it was her own lack of foresight that had left her unprepared.

But Harry had been prepared, Harry was not daunted by anything, even the creeping close of the shadow of death. He was chivalry's champion, fighting for justice and mercy: it was not possible that tomorrow anybody would resist him.

*

As he had said, his appearance at the door of the Greyfriars prison was the signal for an abrupt change of attitude on the part of the gaolers. There were two on duty, a young man and an older one, neither, Harry noted, of very intelligent aspect. At his demand to see the prisoner Thornwood they let him in without question, staring at his fine garments and the sad beauty of the girl beside him. She was wearing one of his sister Meg's best gowns, of black velvet with silver embroidery and a little pearl-embroidered ruff, and looked to them every bit as grand as they imagined the Queen herself to appear.

'Is my servant imprisoned with others?' Harry asked, and was told, 'Nay, sir, alone, we mostly keep condemned heretics so, lest they preach to the rest.' The gaoler laughed as he spoke, but Harry's icy stare cut off his mirth like a knife.

Alan started up from the straw pallet at the opening of the door. Jacquette would hardly have known him, so filthy and haggard he was, and he could hardly believe his eyes at seeing his visitors. They gazed at each other for a moment, then she flew into his arms. As they murmured incoherently, Harry looked round in disgust at the mean, squalid cell. But at least, praised be God, it was a solitary prison, not full of those who might stare and listen.

Alan put Jacquette gently away from him. 'I shall foul your clothes – keep away from me. I stink, this place stinks. It's not fit for either of you.'

'We guessed it might not be wholly fit for you,' Harry said, 'and therefore brought a few necessities. Water and soap, alas, we could not bring.' He displayed what his saddle-pack had held – the food and drink, blankets and clean shirt. Alan's eyes filled with tears. He turned his face against the wall; Jacquette held him, weeping but murmuring comfort, while Harry gazed through the window and took note of the surroundings. If the worst came to the worst . . . but it should not.

While Alan changed his shirt, shudderingly stuffing the old one through the window-bars, then ate and drank wolfishly, Harry talked, outlining his plans. 'I have all the names of all the authorities. They will listen to me, or I'm much mistaken. I would visit them alone, leaving Jacquette with you, but I think even priestly eyes may be more moved by her looks than by mine. Be of good cheer, keep up your heart, trust in God and me.'

'Both,' said Alan, 'but especially you.'

'Hush!' Jacquette glanced round fearfully. 'They'll hear you, and it will sound like more heresy. See, I brought you a Latin missal – it will look well if you are seen to read it. And Harry has money for you to give the gaolers to buy more food and wine.'

'Should I hear that has not been done,' Harry said, 'I will have them punished or dismissed. Now we must go, for the sun is high. I shall get word to you soon, believe me.' He held out his hand, which Alan clasped for a long moment. Jacquette kissed his cheek, and did not wipe off the grime it left on her lips. Then they said their farewell and set out on what would be a strange mission for Harry Brome: to save the life of the man who was mate to the woman he loved.

It was all in vain. Priest, justice, magistrate listened as he politely reasoned, requested, demanded, argued, at last roared like the rampant lion that held up the escutcheon of the Tudors. The Queen's commissioner, they said, would be visiting Reading and Oxford for an important burning, that of Bishop Ridley and Master Latimer. He would not expect to hear news of proven heretics being released. In any case, nobody dare carry such responsibility. There was no further court of appeal. The execution would take place as settled, on the following Monday. Several other heretics would have been convicted by then, and a good crowd could be expected. They wished Sir Harry and his fair companion a very good day and called down various blessings on their heads.

It was almost dusk. They had appointed Harry's man Luke Carter to meet them at a tavern near the abbey, where their horses had been stabled all day. Luke saw by their bearing as they approached him, weary and dejected, that the day had been a failure. Even his proud master seemed to have no more fight left in him.

'Why not take a cup of wine before we set out for home, sir? The inn is a good one and the people will not trouble you.'

'Wine!' Harry said bitterly. 'And drink a toast to damned stiff-necked inhumanity and blinkered bigotry – why not, indeed.' But he followed Luke into a tiny parlour at the back of the tavern's main chamber, where they could see a few drinkers as they passed its door. They sat down on benches in the little room, empty but for themselves. Harry stared gloomily at the wall, and Jacquette put her head in her hands. She wished the wine that was coming might be poisoned, but that was a cowardly wish.

'There is no more to do,' Harry said. 'Tomorrow I ride to London. God send the Queen is there.'

From the room where men were drinking there came to them, light and sweet as a blackbird's song, the notes of a fiddle. The merry country tune came nearer, clearer, and the fiddler himself stood in the doorway. He was a tiny gnomelike man, with an eye as lively as his music.

'Sir Henry Brome, I venture? And the fair dame who lights this place as Venus does the skies, Mistress Thornwood?' He bowed low and gracefully, then without invitation seated himself beside them, in an easy comfortable manner.

'My name, noble sir and gentle mistress, is Davie of Clyro.'

XVIII
The Hands of a Lady

He beamed, as though introducing himself by the most famous name in the world. Harry, in no mood for foolery, said curtly, 'I'll pay you for your music, friend, but not for your conversation.' He threw a coin on the table. The fiddler picked it up, admired and pocketed it. 'Ah,' he said, 'but young madam here, who deals in mysteries, is full of wonder that a wandering fiddler knows your names and estates. Will you not spare old Davie some of your precious time to hear how he came by them – when he tells you it has to do with her husband, poor wretch?'

Jacquette sat up sharply. 'Yes! Tell us anything you can.'

'My throat's indifferent dry, mistress.' The potman had brought their wine; Harry ordered ale for the fiddler, a good large pot of it. If the fellow had anything worth hearing to say, let him talk. But he warned Davie, 'Make your story short – we must be on our way before dusk falls.'

Davie drank deep, smacked his lips, carefully laid his fiddle aside, wrapped in a cloth, and, elbows on table began to talk in his fluent Welsh way, catching his hearers' attention with his first words.

'I was fiddling away, merry as a cricket, look you, last Plough Monday, at the house of a farmer near to Oxford, a good man with an open hand and full moneybags, when there comes to me this lean fellow, garbed black as a crow, that I took for an Oxford scholar. "Know you of the Hooders, fiddler?" he asks me. "A set of mummers having with them a Marian with a sharp tongue and a sharper knife?"'

Jacquette started, catching her breath.

'I misliked him for a rum cully, but he paid handsome, and I'm a poor man, friends. I told him where he might find 'em. And when he was gone I wished my words back, for "Dafydd,"

I said to myself, "who knows but that one means great harm to some poor soul, and if he does it that will be your fault, *bach*." That's what I said to myself, sir, mistress. So because of my doubting, and because I'm curious as a *catti* (which is one of our Welsh words the same as your English one, you may like to know) I travelled to the place where I thought the Hooders might be, and there they were.

'The men were, that's to say, the Robin and the Friar, but not the Marian, she and the Robin having had a fierce fight, and she run away because he'd beat her sore and she was childing and feared for the babe. But I found her easy, and she told me the black crow-man had found her, too, and given her money to talk.'

'I know what she told him,' Jacquette said. The fiddler's eyes twinkled at her.

'Hap you do, and hap I know myself now. Not a pretty tale, indeed.' He went on to tell them how he had taken up with Grizel, out of pity for her discarded state, alone as she was with her small sickly baby, and had found her something tamer now than she had been, weak in body and with a new softness since the birth. The child was all she had ever had of her own; all her fierceness had gone into protecting him, and a kind of change had come over her as happened to some women with the coming of a child.

She had got out of Gideon Baldwin the fact that he meant no good to Alan, and had the wit to find out his name and where he lived, pretending that she might have more information to sell him.

'I never had a wife, see, so a kestrel's all the same to me as a turtledove, and we travel comfortable enough together, Grizel and me, and little Owain. We wintered round about Oxford and the river towns, and found the living soft, so here we stayed, keeping our eyes and ears open; that's how I know without your telling me what has come to your Alun, mistress. (Alun, see, nearly the same name as the English – there's strange.)'

'The whole story is strange,' Harry said. 'I think you must be sent to help us. If your – if Grizel is willing we must meet and talk of what can be done, if anything can.' Jacquette nodded emphatically.

'I will take any chance. Even if Grizel hated me still I would face her, for Alan's sake.'

'We shall not return home tonight,' Harry decided, and dispatched Luke to find them rooms at a reputable inn where he was well known. Davie and Grizel lodged in a hut-dwelling by the river, beyond the town, and there they would meet early the next morning; it would not be safe to be seen together by curious eyes. In the night Harry sometimes doubted his own wisdom in trusting such an odd character as the fiddler, and the good faith of a woman who had once been Jacquette's worst enemy, and still might be. But needs must when the devil drives, and all other means had failed him.

Jacquette hardly recognised the woman who came stooping out of the long low hut which Davie had built. Always thin, Grizel was now skeletal, the cheekbones seeming about to start through the skin. She had aged prematurely, after the manner of her kind. Deep lines and wrinkles marked her brown face, and the long luxuriant hair showed grey streaks. Yet she could not have been much older than Jacquette.

The baby in her arms was wizened, monkey-faced; he had not rounded out into cherubic likeness, and his wail was discontented and came often. When Grizel laid him on the grass it could be seen that he had at least been spared the torture inflicted on babies of a better kind, swaddling-bands.

'This is my mort, Grizel,' Davie said. 'But you two ladies are old acquaintances. Make your curtsey to the gentlefolk, Grizel.'

Curtseying was not Grizel's fashion of greeting. She ducked her head in a sharp bow directed towards Harry, whose appearance dazzled her with its splendour. Jacquette she eyed uncomprehendingly. Could the girl who had stolen her lover and been married by a hedge-priest as beggars do, under a bush, have turned into this fine lady whose skin was as velvet-soft as her spreading gown? Grizel had thought her only a travelling dell like herself, yet now she seemed a princess. And as she had changed, so had Grizel, in her new maternity and her life with Davie. The hatred she had once felt was gone.

Jacquette smiled and held out her hand. Grizel took it in her own grimy one, and their long enmity was over.

'Now,' Harry said, 'we must talk, plan. This is a desperate state of things and needs a cool brain and a bold imagination, or Alan will burn next Monday.'

Grizel shivered. ''Tis a cruel death, the worst of all. I saw it once, couldn't sleep after . . .'

'Shush, woman,' said Davie. 'Five days we have, five days only.'

'Let no one think of gallant rescues on horseback,' Harry warned, 'with so many standing by, and a prisoner bound with chains to a stake, which I hear is what they do. The task would be hopeless.'

'You have servants, though, sir,' Davie said, 'good strong men with some fight in 'em, and maybe guns and pikes?'

'I have, Davie, and if I used them we should all end up in prison. No, it must be subtler than that.'

The curiously-assorted group sat on the cold October ground, over which Davie had thrown a blanket for the guests' better comfort. Jacquette's mind was a blank. She could only pray, and cling to the belief that little Davie had been sent to them for some good purpose, if only to bring hope, however short-lived, to days that would otherwise have held unrelieved dread.

Rooks wheeled overhead in a sky that showed alternate clouds and sunshine, a cow lowed somewhere near, shadows came and went on a half-ruined wall. The least sight or sound seemed to move time on at a giddy pace: another second gone, another minute, soon another hour. And they had only five days.

Harry said abruptly, 'I must go and walk by myself. Something may come to me.' The other three were almost silent, the two women because they could not think what to say to each other, Davie because his alert mind was darting round and round the problem like a swallow catching insects on the wing. The baby cried, and Grizel fed him at her lean breast, though he was of an age to crawl. Jacquette felt sorry for them both, particularly the old-faced child. In the pouch she wore at her waist was the worn wooden angel, the toy of her own infancy, which she still carried from sentiment or superstition. No matter which, there was a better use for it. Taking it out, she showed it to the child, temptingly. He put out a claw tentatively, then withdrew it, being unused to gifts.

'Take it, Owain,' she said, 'there.' She closed the skinny fingers round it, and was rewarded by the beginnings of a toothless smile. Grizel looked alarmed. 'He'll mammock it, my lady.'

'He may keep it to do as he likes with. A child needs toys.'

Then Grizel, too, smiled, a smile almost as toothless as her son's. And at that moment Harry came back, striding towards them through the trees.

'I have thought of a plan,' he said. 'It may work – it must work. But we need all our wits about us, each one of us.' He had no doubts about Davie's wits, more than a few about Grizel's. 'It is like a piece of strategy in war – if one part fails, all fail. We each have a part to play – yours the hardest, Jacquette – and we must play it as though our own lives depended on it, as they may yet. When I have told you what it is, and we have gone over it again and again, until we know it like our own names, Jacquette and I will go home to Brome Court.'

'I want to stay near Alan,' Jacquette said.

'And be noticed, and make them wonder why you stay? No, you go with me. You, Davie, go about the town and be our eyes and ears, to find out such things as the time this – ceremony – is to take place on Monday, and what gaolers will be in attendance at the prison, and if a priest is to be sent there. Listen, now.'

They listened. An hour later they were still listening, each of them now able to recite his or her own part in the plan. Jacquette's heart sank lower and lower. It seemed so ambitious, so chancy, depending on others doing what they might be expected to do and circumstances being favourable in every aspect, which seemed most unlikely.

She was further depressed, after they had left Davie and Grizel, to find that Harry also had serious doubts. 'I shall go to London as I planned, just in case I am able to see Her Majesty and she is merciful; then there would be no need for any rescue.'

'You said you were riding home with me –'

'So as not to alarm them. A baronet may look at a queen, I suppose, like the cat in the adage, but to them it would seem like paying a visit to God. Luke shall go home with you, and you'll see me as soon as I can get back. Keep up your heart.' He kissed her hand and mounted the noble Casimir, who had spirit and strength enough to carry his master the full forty miles if need be, but it would not be asked of him.

When Harry returned it was late on Saturday, only one day's grace remaining. He was weary, stiff and travel-stained, and his face told Jacquette how he had fared. To the others he said little, for three can keep a secret if two are away, as the country saying went. They knew of his visit to London, but nothing of the plan for Monday.

'It was worse than I feared. Her Court is like a tomb since Philip went back to Spain, all gloom and black clothing, as though someone had died. So they have – plenty! by her orders – but not Philip; he merely snatched at a political straw to get away from his wife. And what a wife!'

'What is she like?'

'I wish I need not remember. Her face is almost a square, with a great bald brow above, her skin fair-coloured enough but crumpled like a ball of paper, her eyes sharp, for she sees badly and stares, and her mouth like a trap. Her body is skin and bones and her voice gruff as a man's. Can you wonder Philip ran back to Spain?'

'No. But your petition?'

'She curled her lips – what there was of them,' said the normally chivalrous Harry bitterly, 'and asked me if I would like to think of my servant's soul in hell-flames for all eternity. "What is a little cleansing fire here on earth," she asked me, "compared with that? You would be kind to be cruel, I am cruel to be kind." And I could not answer her, she was not to be reasoned with or argued with. I knelt there like a gawping fool and listened to that mad bitch growling her pious platitudes at me, and dare not answer back for fear of my own skin.'

'You could undo us all with words like that, brother,' Simon said.

'I only dare say them between these walls. A mad bitch she is, and should be hanged for one. I am sick to think any of her blood flows in my veins.' He rose abruptly and went out of the great hall, and they heard him clattering up the stairs. Agnes shook her head. 'All so unlike our Harry. I've known him wince and say nothing when one of the maids spilt near-boiling water over him – because he wouldn't speak harsh to a woman. And now to call the Queen . . . fie!'

He is fire and ice, steel and velvet, thought Jacquette. I know the elements that make him up; I know him better than Alan, better than myself. My heart is a palace wherein he may be. And he may unlock it without any key . . . But the time is not now, perhaps not ever.

They went back to Reading on Sunday, staying at the same inn, and again with Luke beside them. He had been let into his master's confidence, and wore a very solemn face, feeling his responsibility. Alan had not been a servant as he and his fellows had, but the sense of it was the same, and they had all liked him, a quiet, clever fellow with no outlandish ways. As to burning a living creature, Protestant or Catholic or pagan, it was all one, there was no warranty for it in God's book or man's and Luke would have ventured himself on this errand even if the man he was trying to save had been a black-hearted villain.

On the journey a terrible thought struck Jacquette. She turned to Harry a face drained of colour.

'What if they've changed the day? What if . . . the thing is done?'

'It will not have been. The rain has been heavy today and rain is not the right weather. What a year for rain!' He glanced up at the black clouds. 'Storms, floods, hail and lately a meteor in the skies. Someone is angry.'

But the next morning was bright and clear. Harry rose at first light and sent a maid to wake Jacquette, but she had not slept. They must wait some time yet, since the fire was not to be lit until ten o'clock, so that it could be over by dinner-time, said Davie when he presented himself at their inn. There would be a priest in the market place, not at the prison, and the two gaolers they had seen before would escort the prisoner.

Nervous and tense, Jacquette and Harry walked about the town. Harry was inconspicuously dressed like a countryman, and had left his chin unshaven, and Jacquette wore a plain black cloak and her hair bundled into a cap. They stopped sometimes to chat with people going about their business, and were agreeably surprised to get much the same reply each time to their question: 'Will you go to see the heretic burned this morning?'

'That I shan't – a sin and a shame. How should a decent body's eyes bear such a sight?' and the questioned one would scurry on its way.

'But,' said Harry, 'there will be many who do go. Something in the human composition is drawn to the horrible, when it is happening to somebody else.'

'I wonder they can talk to us and not hear my heart beating – it sounds to me as loud as a drum. What time is it?'

'Close on nine by the last church clock.'

'Then the time is coming.'

'Yes, soon.'

They were like soldiers waiting for the word to charge. As the low sun rose higher in the heavens, and nine chimes sounded close by, Jacquette suddenly felt all fear leave her. Harry seemed to sense the exact moment when this happened, for he looked down at her and took her hand in a warm, strong, comradely grasp. *'Coragio,'* he said.

They spoke little as they walked by the side of the little River Kennet towards the market place. When they reached it, a crowd was already gathering, folk standing about talking, some staring at the faggots two executioners were piling up in the centre, each one a bundle of sticks tied with rope at either end. A barrel of tar was beside them. The stake was a tall thick post sunk into the ground. Nearby a small fire was burning briskly.

'They say there was much ado to keep the wood dry in yesterday's rain,' Jacquette overheard. 'That's bad, for it'll burn slow and draw out the agony.'

'Ah, poor soul.'

'Is there to be more than one?'

'Nay, they couldn't find more, but they say the Queen must have one a week, so this lad must burn by himself.'

'Who is it?'

'Some fellow from Henley way.'

'Diables, barbares!' Jacquette hissed. 'I should like to see *them* face it.'

'Aye. When He said "Father, forgive them, for they know not

what they do" even He can hardly have thought the day would come when they'd do it in His name. Look, Davie's at work.'

It had been arranged that Davie and Grizel should between them distract the crowd's attention from the main entertainment, and here was Davie, in his best holiday gear, tuning up his fiddle to play as he had never played before, even on May Day or Twelfth Night. By way of warming up his audience he strolled from one group to another, twisting his nutcracker face into comic grimaces and telling outrageous jokes that brought shrieks of delighted laughter. At the same time he watched Grizel out of the corner of his eye as she prepared for her part in the plan. Owain had been left with some of Grizel's family. She wore the red dress in which Jacquette had first seen her play Maid Marian, and a patchwork shawl over it, bright-coloured wooden beads round her neck, and her hair, well brushed for once, flowing to her waist. She looked almost handsome, certainly arresting enough to draw men's eyes.

Half-past nine. Harry strolled towards Grizel, lifted his cap and bowed. It was the signal: she gave an almost imperceptible nod, and began to turn the handle of the hurdy-gurdy she was carrying, at the same time raising her powerful voice in the ballad of 'Henry my Son', which everyone knew but which was so dramatic that no one could resist listening to the end of it, where the poisoned Henry bequeathed his sweetheart a 'rope to hang her, Mother.' It seemed suitable for the occasion.

Swiftly Harry made the agreed signal to Davie, who, his fiddle already tuned, launched into a lively air which brought reproving looks from the graver-minded among the crowd, and then stern rebuke from the guards in charge of the execution. It was all useful distraction.

They were almost at the door of the Greyfriars prison, where they halted for their last, fateful conference.

'You think you can do it?' Harry asked Jacquette.

She drew aside her cloak and showed the wrenching-iron she was carrying. 'With this.'

'I shall be waiting where we appointed. God keep you.' A quick grasp of her hand, and he was gone, round the side of the building towards the monks' graveyard. Jacquette drew a deep breath and knocked at the prison door.

The younger gaoler opened it.

'I would see my husband for the last time,' she said, putting a coin into the man's already outstretched hand.

'Aye, mistress, I'll let you in.' It was the custom to allow such visits, out of common compassion, and the gaolers remembered with pleasure the money Harry had given them. He led her to the cell door. 'Very quiet, 'e's been, no trouble. You'll be swift, mistress.'

'Yes.'

Alan was pacing the cell, almost at breaking-point. He knew the plan, set out in a note from Harry, which had arrived in the cell tied to a stone; Davie had pushed it in through the window. Jacquette hugged him briefly.

'Listen to me. Pray aloud, in Latin if you can remember any, if not throw in some Latin words, while I get to work.'

There was no time to think of prayers. Alan gabbled the first thing that came into his head, which happened to be the old charm he had been unable to remember at his trial. Ironically, it came back to him perfectly now.

> *'Sanguis mane in te, sicut fecit Christus in me,*
> *Sanguis mane in tua vena, sicut Christus in sua poena;*
> *Sanguis mane fixus, sicut Christus quando fuit crucifixus.'*

Jacquette, while he chanted the same words over and over again, worked feverishly on the window-bars with the wrenching-iron. They were rusty, stout and ancient, fixed in place perhaps sixty years before. She attacked them from top to bottom, using both her hands, trying to force the iron to bend, to widen the distance between the bars. But they would not yield, not the least fraction, and she began to break out in a cold sweat. Alan, behind her, applied his own hands, but they were prison-weakened and no more successful. Jacquette gasped, 'Jesu Maria! we're undone.' Alan's sobbing breaths were in her ear and she felt him shaking from head to foot.

'Give it up,' he said. 'I knew it was hopeless. God!' He began to weep.

Jacquette shook her head. For a moment she let herself rest, then, using her bare hands and summoning all her strength, grasped the base of one bar and pulled. Amazingly, miraculously, it broke away from the stone, worn by rust as it was at that point.

Smothering a cry of triumph, she attacked the other bar, where she now saw the same weakness. It gave, enough to be pushed outwards. Alan's hands on hers, they pressed out the first bar, which snapped at its top end.

They turned on each other faces of incredulous joy.

'*Now*,' Jacquette said. 'Step on my back.' She dropped on all fours. 'Say nothing. I shall not be hurt. Oh, hurry!'

For a moment his full weight was on her, spine-cracking, as he stretched up to force his body through the window-space. Where shoulders can go the rest can follow, and he was thin and lithe. Then with blessed relief the weight was lifted and he was wriggling through the window. She straightened up in time to see that he had landed awkwardly on the grass among the small gravestones, and that Harry was there, raising him, rushing him away towards the narrow ginnel that ran alongside the old windowless house.

A burning pain made her look down at her hands. They were raw, bleeding, the skin rubbed off palms and fingers, an ugly sight. Wrapping her cloak round her so that they were invisible, she raised her voice in a tearful farewell, mingling endearments with sobs. Enough, not too much, for now she must distract the gaolers.

She left the cell, which had not been re-locked, for how should any prisoner escape, with his escort waiting outside? The men, who had been hovering, looked relieved at her reappearance.

'Make haste, mistress. Time to be gone.'

She gave them the full benefit of her eyes, huge and tragic in an emotion-ravaged face.

'Good sirs, give us your prayers. Both of us. Say a *Paternoster* for his soul with me. It will bring you forgiveness for what you must do.'

They exchanged doubtful looks, but gabbled the prayer together.

'I thank you from my heart. Gentle souls, I have a sort of spirit of prophecy on me – sometimes it comes in time of sore trouble. May I counsel you for your own good?'

Even men with a solemn errand ahead of them could not resist such a personal offer from the beautiful sad near-widow who was, if they had but known it, using every ounce of her professional training and the magnetism that had come down to her in the blood of the *trouvères*, charmers of kings. To the older man she said, slowly, gravely, 'Use mercy, and mercy shall be shown to thee in thy most need. Remember this.' The man nodded, deeply impressed. She turned to the younger one, wishing she dare touch him for better effect, but her wounded hands must stay hidden.

'Young one, thou wilt ever be lucky and prosperous. Only take counsel from women, not men, and all will be well with thee. Say an *Ave*, a *Paternoster* and a *Gloria* each night before sleeping. I will pray . . . ah!' With a moan, she slipped to the ground and lay motionless, her eyes shut.

Ten o'clock was chiming from the church tower. The older gaoler cursed.

'Plague on the wench to go swounding now – we'll be beaten for this.' But she lay between them and the cell door, and they could hardly kick her aside or invite the prisoner to step over her.

'Give us a hand to bear her into the air.' This was exactly what Jacquette wanted. She made herself heavy in their arms, still apparently unconscious, keeping her hands by her sides and hoping blood would not seep through her cloak.

They laid her down on a flat tombstone outside the door and went back into the prison. Opening her eyes, she saw that a crowd had gathered expectantly, hoping to march in the procession of death. Sliding off the stone, she bunched up her skirts and dashed through the waiting people. Some stared after her, but none tried to stop her, their attention being on the prison.

Greyfriars was almost at a crossroads. She hesitated briefly, then took the street opposite to the one leading to the market-place, and ran like the wind, glancing back sometimes to see if there were pursuers. Distant shouts came from Greyfriars; the escape had been discovered.

After some quarter of a mile she changed direction to go north-east, towards the river, along a lane and through fields, finding her way by the sun, and thankful that it shone. Now she kept up a steady pace, neither run nor walk, to ease the pressure on her lungs.

At last a line of willows came in sight. She had almost reached the river-side. Gaining it, she saw a wrecked boat moored by the bank, a landmark Davie had pointed out. Another hundred yards east, and there was the hut where he lived; and beside it three men looking eagerly towards her – Harry, Luke and Alan.

XIX
Go thy ways for me

They hurried to meet her and she fell breathless into their arms, embraced by one after another. 'Well done! Oh, bravely done!' Harry said.

'I thought – it would not – be done at all,' Jacquette gasped. 'Those accursed bars . . .' She gave a suppressed shriek as Alan took her hand and exclaimed in horror at what the bars had done.

'It's nothing – it will mend. But you! Oh, what a change!'

It had been decided that Alan must at all costs be disguised. He was to go with Grizel to the Romany camp where some of Grizel's relations were and where Owain was being cared for. The offer of gold had reconciled them to the idea of taking in a *gorgio*, but it was as well for him to look as much like them as possible. Luke had hastily and roughly shaved him and stained his face with umber, dark brown earth mixed to a paste with water, already prepared. A flop-brimmed countryman's hat, with a sprig of rowan-berries pinned on it, a gaudy yellow scarf and a patched, torn jacket completed the transformation, and a shabby, scabby horse without saddle or bridle awaited, grazing with the others.

But Grizel had not come back from the town. She and Davie had been told to stay there as long as they could, providing distraction and confusion that would help to cover Alan's escape. Harry watched the sun anxiously.

'You should be gone by now – the search will be widening. Where the plague have they got to?'

'I could go alone, and try to find the place,' Alan suggested.

'On that nag? You could never manage it saddleless as Grizel could. And you, Jacquette, we must get you away. If you went back to Brome they'd be on you like hounds – no, it must be as we planned, you must go to John Berkeley at Esher. He expects you, the tale's been put about that you're a maidservant in need of a place, sent to his wife by Agnes. Luke knows the way and the house. I see no hindrance, do you?'

'No . . . But I would see Alan away first.'

Luke, long-sighted, was pointing across a field. 'There they be.' To everyone's relief Davie and Grizel were to be seen hurrying towards them, Davie waving his fiddle and grinning broadly.

'It went all to plan, very perfect,' he told them. 'When the word got about in the market place we took ourselves off to Greyfriars, and there we drew as many eyes as we could. The gaolers ran about like hens with their heads cut off. I bawled out that I'd seen the prisoner skulking down a ginnel. They made haste to where I said. Grizel faked the prettiest fit you ever saw, foaming at the mouth with soap-bubbles, enough to melt the heart of a magistrate. I begged them to help her, only I used the Welsh to maze them the more then, when all was Bedlam, me and my bonny rumpscuttle hastened away. The Festival of All Fools it was, my masters, St Zany's Day.' He performed a small dance of triumph.

'You did well, both of you,' Harry said. 'You shall be rewarded. But now you must go, Grizel, at once. You know what to do?'

She nodded and disappeared into the hut, emerging in a brown dress instead of the conspicuous red one, with a shawl hiding her hair. Alan helped her to mount the nag, at which gallantry she stared, then shook hands with Harry and Luke. 'Gratitude's a poor word. How can I thank you all for my life?'

'By getting safe away, and quickly, that's thanks in plenty,' said Harry. 'Go now.'

Alan embraced Jacquette, holding her tightly for a moment. 'I'll get word to you. Farewell, sweetheart.'

'God keep you,' she said. He mounted behind Grizel, clasping her waist. She jerked the rough strip of leather which served both for bridle and bit, and the horse moved off at a surprising pace. Jacquette would have watched it out of sight, but Harry was propelling her to her own mount. She had hoped for a clasp, a touch, a farewell kiss as was the custom: but he swung her up into the saddle and stood by the stirrup, his eyes holding hers, saying what might not be said in words. She put her torn fingers to her lips, then, painfully, took the reins. Harry spoke briefly to Luke before mounting his own horse and riding off, without a backward look.

They were all gone but Davie. He gazed after them with an enigmatic smile that hid his bright eyes among their wrinkles. Picking up his fiddle, he launched into a tune popular with the crowds, and gleefully sang the words:

> 'Farewell, dear Love, since this I find is true,
> I will not spend more time in wooing you.
>   But seeing I must lose
>   Thy love which I did choose,
>   Go thy ways for me,
>   Since it may not be.
> Go thy ways for me. But whither?
> Go – O, but where I may come thither!'

The home of Sir John Berkeley and his family was the best house in Esher village after the manor house, Esher Place, and like it stood on low ground near the River Mole. It was small compared with Brome Court, yet finely proportioned, having been built only in King Henry's reign, with tall many-paned windows and elaborate ceilings of plaster-work. In appearance it lacked nothing, in atmosphere everything, for it was all-pervadingly, incurably damp. The nearby river seemed to have extended itself to seep up through floors, trickle down walls, rot wood and cause great patches on walls. If a warming-pan were thrust between the sheets, steam would rise from them. Old bones there ached at the thought of contracting ague, rheumatism and lung-rot, young ones shivered with the fear of becoming bent and crooked before their time.

Jacquette, while not afraid for her limbs or lungs, disliked the place intensely. John Berkeley had made her very welcome, for his friend Harry's sake and her own; he had noticed her with keen admiration on his visit to Brome Court, and though Harry had not risked giving him details in a letter, he knew that she had done something notable to rescue a victim of the Queen's persecution. She was known by the name of Valencey, to avoid all connection with Alan.

His wife Cecily was not so welcoming. Vain as only a really plain woman can be, she was pleased to add a maid to her household who was skilled at dressing her hair in elaborate styles. Cecily also valued Jacquette's ability to heighten her complexion skilfully with a touch of red salve, to darken her almost invisible eyebrows and lengthen her eyes with moistened soot. But she was less pleased to be in constant proximity to a young woman of such unusual and exotic beauty, with a pretty French voice that allured the men. Not only that, Jacquette could play the lute better than she did, and also read and write with ease.

Jacquette received more complaints, even blows and pinches, than the other maids, and had to bear them in silence for safety's sake. Life was dull, besides. She was not required to entertain; Cecily Berkeley had been told nothing of her skills, other than that she could play and sing well. The days were a tedious round of family-prayers, still-room duties, sewing, mending and embroidery with the other maids and their mistress, readings aloud from devotional books (John's great-uncle was a bishop, who must not call and catch the women engaged in frivolity), more prayers, and bed in a dormitory shared with six other girls. Sometimes she yawned until her jaws seemed about to crack. The only compensation was that her duties did not include attendance in the nurseries, where Cecily's five children (she had been married at fifteen) always seemed to be in the throes of one illness or another.

She thought constantly of Harry. She had heard nothing of him; he might have been dead for all she knew. But when anxiety drove her into asking John, he said that Harry was perfectly well, but had been arrested after Alan's escape on strong suspicion of having been involved in it. He had been imprisoned for almost two months in Oxford's prison, the Bocardo, where Archbishop Cranmer waited for death. Suspicion of Harry hung largely upon his visit to the Queen to intercede for Alan. But nothing could be proved, and they had let him go.

He might have told me of this, Jacquette thought; he might have sent me a word. It had been all a dream and an illusion, what had seemed to happen the day he rescued her from Baldwin.

It was only a young man's brief lust for a woman who belonged to another, and was therefore not for him, an honourable gentleman. Jacquette wished he had not been so honourable. For so long she had lived like a nun; it would have been pleasant to have something to remember, to live over again in the long winter nights, amid damp sheets and the snuffling of maids with bad colds.

She thought of Alan, too, but in a strangely remote way. He had been distant from her in spirit long before their physical parting. Now he was almost a ghost in her memory, the ghost he would have been in truth if the Reading plot had gone wrong. 'At least I can be thankful for that,' she told herself. 'When I am old and ugly and bent double with rheumatism I can tell my grandchildren I once saved a life. Only there will be no grandchildren to tell: it will have to be the kitchen cat, and she will tell her kittens, and so the legend of Jacquette will go down in history.'

A shrill voice broke into her musing. 'Valencey! where are you, lazy slut? Idling again?'

'Coming, madam.' Another hour to spend painting Cecily's doughy little face, and after that a half-hour of reading from the Prophet Ezekiel, and another patient enduring of the maid Susannah's distracted fears that the whole household would catch the spotted fever, which was at present raging in the nurseries. Oh life, oh time . . .

The monotony was broken one wintry morning when a messenger brought a letter addressed to Mistress Valencey. He had come to the door used by servants and tradesmen, and nobody had taken much notice of him. A shabby-dressed fellow, they thought, a tatterdemalion. But the letter was written on good enough paper and sealed securely. Jacquette knew the writing; it was the hand she had longed to see, and she burned to read it. The hour of needlework in Cecily's parlour seemed a century, before she could slip away to read it alone. She tore off the seal, and disappointment overwhelmed her: it was not from Harry, he had only written the superscription.

> My dear lady, this comes to apprise you that I am well and safe, which but for you would be far otherwise. I trust you

to be the same wherever you may be, which I do not know and therefore send this to Sir Harry who will despatch it to you. Where I am cannot concern you, but I live the free life again as I longed to do. Jacquette, the best thanks I can give you for all your great benefits to me is to unloose the bond between us. I have found the *patrico* who performed the ceremony, and he was never in holy orders but a false priest. That we were handfasted is no binding tie to such as us, though it might weigh if we were royal or noble. If you should love elsewhere I would not stand in the way, so I sign myself in all kind affection, no longer your husband but your loving friend and debtor for life, with my blessings.

A.T.

Jacquette laid the letter down with conflicting feelings. She was free of Alan and grateful that he had taken this generous way of releasing her. She rejoiced that he also was free, and happy in his way. Yet the knowledge that he was no longer part of her life made her strangely forlorn. Now she was truly alone. She wept bitterly and long, and when she returned to her mistress's presence Cecily remarked tartly that it would be better if servants did not receive letters, since they produced such an ugly swelling of the eyes.

Harry too had received a letter, delivered to him by the same ragged messenger. In it Alan asked him to send the other to Jacquette, and gave him the same information: that they had never been married, though they had thought so in all good faith, and that she would now greatly need a friend. Delicately, Alan added no more.

Harry ordered that the messenger be fed, rewarded and sent on his way to Esher. Then he climbed the twisting stair to the housekeeper's parlour, where Dorothy and a sewing-maid worked at a robe for Agnes's new baby. At the sight of his face Dorothy murmured to the girl to make herself scarce.

'Now, my dear, what ails you?' She had been a surrogate mother to Harry and Simon for so long that she needed no telling when either was in trouble.

'This.' He showed her the letter, but she smilingly shook her head. 'I am not learnèd – read it to me.'

After hearing the contents, she nodded contentedly. 'I thought as much. So what is your trouble, Hal?'

'Why, it tears me apart. With all my heart I long to go to her I am deep in love with her, though you were not to know that.

Dorothy shook with laughter. 'Do you take me for a fool lad, or a blind old beldam? It was written all over you as clear as clear, for the whole house to see if it took the pains to look. I shouldn't wonder if Nick and Elizabeth prattle of it, how their Uncle Harry goes about like a cow that has lost her calf. And the girl is in the same case, I can see that. Give us the credit for some sense, if you have none yourself, as I think, for else why are you frittering time away up here, when you could be on the road to Esher? I see no frost or snow, but a very fine day for riding.'

'How can you talk so? Since I can't marry Jacquette there's no purpose in going to her.' He flung himself moodily into a chair, the scowl of a thwarted Tudor darkening his face. Dorothy critically examined the fine stitching of the infant's robe.

'Since you can't marry her . . . Has your great longing been to make her your paramour, then? I should have thought the girl deserved better, after one marriage that was not a marriage.

'You know that was never in my mind! I mean that I have vowed never to marry, since I caused Joan's death. I have said it a thousand times.'

Dorothy glanced heavenwards. 'Give me patience! It was not you who caused poor Joan's death, but God, or Dame Nature or who you will. There was some obstruction in her which would not let the babe be born, and so both died. Your conscience is too tender, son.'

'It was I who gave her the babe, as though my manhood had been a spear to wound and kill her. The same might happen again, to another wife.'

Dorothy, with a great urge to box his ears, continued to sew 'Has it happened to Simon's wife? She's borne four now, and is more buxom and blooming than ever.'

'Agnes is strong.'

'And Jacquette is not, after she has done more, and suffered more, than Agnes ever did? I see no sign of weakness in her. Moreover, she is a woman grown, and more – she must have, let me see, twenty-three or twenty-four years. Joan was almost a child. Time is speeding on for Jacquette, if she is to bear your sons and daughters, Hal.' Dorothy was sewing rapidly, her eyes on her work, not on Harry's face. 'And I tell you something: I would have suffered the pains of hell to bear a child to your father, even outside wedlock, even though I'd have been openly called a whore for it by those who only smiled behind their hands when they named me his housekeeper. Do you know what I felt when yet another of his bastards ran about this place, tending the fowls or playing with the hounds? I wept, Hal, every time, and there was a great bitterness in my heart, though he never saw it. But I was barren, and now I shall never hold my own babe – or, it seems, yours. So be it, I am condemned.'

This, the longest speech he had ever heard Dorothy make, struck Harry silent. He had indeed never thought of any of these things. They came home to him now with singular force.

Dorothy watched his face, that she knew so well, reading the changes that were going on in his mind. She had opened one door to her obstinate child, but another remained shut, or at the least only a very little way open, and it lay beyond the first door.

'So, now that I have made you see sense (for which poor Joan's ghost will surely thank me) shall we debate what the world will say when you offer Jacquette marriage? You must have thought of that, but all these megrims about the perils of childbed have shielded you from tackling to it.' A startled glance told her that she had guessed right.

'And what will the world say? A few will snigger, like Madam You-know-who at Pangbourne and the Letsworths that think themselves so grand, and will make mirth over the wedding of a Brome to a dancing-girl. But they'll also remember that the Bromes have ever been known as a mad-brained lot, not least my dear Sir Nicholas, and came from no great stock in the first place. Was it not a merchant Brome who built this place, with money got by sharp trading overseas? For the Tudor streak, it's on the wrong side of the blanket and counts little.'

'I hate it,' Harry said. 'I would drain it out of my veins if I could.'

'Let that flea stick on the wall, my dear lad; you'd spill the good sort along with the bad. You should not fear to pass it down to your son, neither, since only the looks are Tudor, the blood itself being Plantagenet. There! am I not an old wiseacre?'

'You are. Very wise.'

Dorothy knew that she was winning. 'As to the neighbourhood talk, those folk who would mock you would do it only for a little, remembering that unless they greeted Jacquette as your lawful lady they'd get no more hospitality here – and that would please 'em not at all. And, Hal, could any point the finger at her and swear that she is not as handsome and fine a lady as any on the banks of Thames? She has all the graces, is learnèd and accomplished and can suit her manners to her company. Once your wife, I'll warrant she'll never be seen again in a skirt that ends above her ankles, or sing one of her ballads of bawdry. No, she will do what's proper to Lady Brome, and nothing more.'

Harry smiled, ruefully. 'Yet I hope she will still be merry. I would not have her lose that, my Merrymaid, for all the airs and graces in the world.'

'You fear that, knowing her as you do?'

'I fear nothing about her, now.'

Dorothy breathed out a sigh of immense relief. 'Then you know what you must do.'

Looking at the woman who had been in the place of a mother to him, it seemed as though light streamed from her bent, comely head, changing his life. He said wonderingly, 'That silk should turn to roses in your lap, madam.'

She looked up, startled. 'What?'

'An old story of a saint . . . Saint Dorothy, as it chances.' He leapt to his feet. 'It is truly a fine day for riding.' He kissed her hand, and was gone out of the room, and the house, like a whirlwind.

Dorothy smiled, and began to feather-stitch the petals of a flower into the robe's design; it was a Tudor rose.

'Can you not sing something more cheerful, Valencey?' Cecily asked peevishly. 'Cold Disdain – Beauty's Tomb – quenchless fires and sable hearses – would you have us more in the dumps than we are, my husband kept from me by the snows in London, no fish to eat this Friday when the bishop comes, and half of us down with spotted fever? I swear you had a bad teacher if such mopish mumpings are all you know.'

Jacquette murmured humbly that she was sorry, she would try to remember something livelier, but every lyric that came into her head seemed more doleful than the last. To pacify her demanding lady she played the first phrases of a pleasant *Branles*, a dance for country or court, then found that she had forgotten the rest. Helplessly she struck random notes, while Cecily munched sweetmeats, wearing a sulky face. To Jacquette's relief a servant appeared. With luck yet another domestic calamity had occurred.

'A gentleman waits below, madam,' he said.

'Then bring him up, dolt.'

'He asks for Mistress Valencey, please you.'

It did not please Cecily at all. She glared. 'Who is this gentleman?'

'Sir John's friend, my lady – Sir Harry Brome.'

Jacquette turned white, then red. Her lute fell to the ground with a clatter, her hands shaking too much to retrieve it. The maids grouped around Cecily gawped and whispered, until their mistress said sharply, 'Where are your manners, wench? You are asked for, go.'

He waited near the stair-foot, a winter prince whose garments sparkled with snow whiter than the knot of pearls in his cap, his face alight with joyous anticipation. In her rush down the staircase Jacquette missed the last two steps and fell, to be caught up in Harry's arms and held there, close and safe. They said nothing, only kissed over and over again and murmured incoherently. The story would wait – what mattered was that he was here at last to claim her.

Of all the things he might have said, a sentence of Scripture came aptly into his mind. Looking down with all his heart in his eyes at her happy face, he said, ' "I would lead thee, and bring thee to my mother's house." '